UNDERNEATH THE MOON

3

DAN HOLT

Published by:

MaxHoltMedia

DAN HOLT

UNDERNEATH THE MOON 3

© 2016 by Dan Holt

Published by Max Holt Media
303 Cascabel Place, Mount Juliet, TN 37122
www.maxholtmedia.com

Other books by Dan Holt: SLEEP MODE, UNDERNEATH THE MOON, UNDERNEATH THE MOON 2 and KEEPSAKE

Cover Design: Max Holt Media & Eddie Holt

Cover art by: ID 49926608 © Rfischia | Dreamstime.com (Earth and Moon)

ISBN 13: 978-1-944537-18-0

DAN HOLT

CONTENTS

DAN HOLT

PROLOGUE

President Howell and his staff sat on the access road and looked across the four-square-mile plot of ground that was to become Giant City, Kansas. The giants, seven times the size of an average man, were busy about the task of laying out the foundations of their homes, school, clinic, super market, and a maintenance-utilities-support, and hardware-store combination; all scaled to their size. They seemed quite happy and content. They had needed their hands and minds tied to something tangible for some time.

The giants, 1212 students, the equivalent of teenagers 14 to 16 years of age, and 4 adult Counselors, were discovered in suspended animation in an underground tunnel on the Moon. A crew of researchers, armed with new space flight technology, discovered the group of survivors while investigating artifacts revealed by a search of the many Apollo photographs. It was learned that the forty-foot-tall humanoids were survivors of an ancient disaster, the explosion of their home planet, as a result of an experiment with hyper-dimensional energy, gone wrong. The civilization, in a last gallant effort, managed to save these youths.

The giants were awakened, brought to Earth, then housed in temporary dwellings near Aurora, Illinois. It was a fabricated Circus Tent City designated as Giant City, Illinois. Soon after the youths were settled, then exercised in regulated therapy sessions, they began to recover their normal strength and well-being. Not long after that they began to show discontent with the strictly regulated living.

The government, recognizing a growing problem, arranged a permanent location, and the construction of a town scaled to their size and needs. A four-square-mile area just outside Wichita, Kansas was chosen for the project. In a clever move on the President's part, he arranged to move the temporary dwellings from Aurora to the site in Kansas and commission the giants to build their own city; with the help of government supplied civil engineers.

Chapter 1

MISSION PLANNING

The White House

Two weeks after the giants were moved to Wichita, Kansas and assigned the task of constructing their own city, President Walter Howell called a special *Meeting of the Minds*. In attendance was the crew of Discovery, NASA, the anthropologist team, the team of linguist, and finally, the Congressional Appropriations Committee on Space Flight.

President Howell stepped to the podium. "Ladies and gentlemen, on the matter of the giants; as most of you know, we have already seen the seeds of unrest begin to surface. However, we have been able to address the problem, at least for a few months, by having the giant population go about arranging their own place to live while we seek permanent answers. I've asked Winston Stone, NASA Administrator, to give us a summary of where we are now in this saga that began with Apollo. Winston...."

Winston Stone went to the podium, placed several sheets of notes on it and began. "The Chicago Linguistics Institute is studying the hundreds of books acquired from the lab discovered underground on the Moon. Bit-by-bit the facts are surfacing, giving us a clearer picture of who the giants are, where they came from, and what they're doing here. Karen Hastings, linguist, Jean Henson, and two assistants have been diligently working directly with the giants to develop better and better communication.

Also, Della Clayton, linguist, and her team are continuing to work on the writings discovered on the Moon. When they began studying the collection of books from a library located on the surface, in a basement of a building that was in ruins, they found that The Library was not to study the Solar System as we originally thought; but to study what was *going on* in the Solar System. We now have reams of data which lead us to believe the following in this saga of the giants. Some fifty thousand years ago the Solar System was home to four livable planets; all blue and white worlds like Earth is now. They were Venus, Earth, Mars, and Solaris 4; now the Asteroid Belt. It is referred to as Solaris 4 instead of Solaris 5 because the planet Mercury was a moon at that time; a moon of Solaris 4, leaving Venus as the first planet from the Sun.

"I don't believe this race of giants evolved on Solaris 4. I think they came here from somewhere outside the Solar System; more than likely Alpha Centauri, the closest star."

Senator James Whitmore, Chair of the Appropriations Committee, raised his hand. The professor paused and raised his eyebrows.

"What makes you think they came from somewhere else?"

"I heard Mentar speaking to the student body, the giants, during their adjustment time to Earth's gravity. Many of the students were full of questions as their strength began to grow and they became more comfortable in Earth's gravity well. He spoke of some ancient writings of their civilization which told of their ancestors coming to Solaris 4 from the stars. They came, the ancient writings said, from a world with two Suns. As most of you know, Alpha Centauri is a binary star system; Centauri A and B. And then there's a red dwarf that's believed to circle the two at a remote distance. Since this star system is the closest, it seems to be the likely location of the *world with two Suns*.

"After they settled here on Solaris 4, over time, a lot of time, their civilization began to divide into two factions. The dominate one was the technical types, the scientists. The other, were nature types, sort of spiritual types, not unlike Earth's native Americans. It

11

finally came to a head and they separated. The nature types, by agreement, moved to Venus; known to them as Solaris 1. Because of its orbit, the planet was very tropical. It had natural features that kept its temperature under control and that faction adjusted to it and lived close to nature, careful not to overtax the natural bounty of the planet. The techs, the scientists, governed on Solaris 4, building a society that was science-oriented and functioned in an environment of socialism. Over time there arose a movement to go home—back to the stars. It became the government's theme.

"They were going to great length to prepare to leave the Solar System. Everything they were doing was focused to that end. We have bits of evidence that they were constructing, or perhaps restoring, a huge space vehicle of some sort that's now in orbit around Saturn; something we will have to check out at a later time. According to one of the four mature giants, they were experimenting with hyper-dimensional energy to power this interstellar vehicle and somehow let the genie out of the bottle and caused the planet to explode. That horrific mistake and subsequent release of billions of comets and asteroids destroyed all the livable worlds of the Solar System except Earth. Only the ancient cave dwellers survived on Earth.

"When the giants in the Arcology on the Moon learned of the scope of the explosion of their home planet, they chose to save the students, the young, from Solaris 4. They had very little time so they used the equipment that they were developing for the interstellar journey to save these students, the ones we found on the Moon.

"The lab on the Moon, no doubt, has many more answers waiting for our investigators. We know so far that they were working on equipment for putting themselves into suspended animation for the journey to the stars. According to the giants, there's a lab also on Mars that was engaged in their effort to put together an enormous starship and go to, or, I think, *return* to the Stars. What would they be working on there on Mars? This was not just a space program but a total effort. We are planning a Mission to Mars immediately and will take two of the Counselors and a representative group of a dozen or so of the student body with us. The rest of the students will see that as a gesture of good will. We'll install radio equipment on Deck 4 of Discovery and at Giant City, Kansas and allow the giants to communicate with their own during the Mission. Additionally, we will modify the Guppy ships to better transport the giants. The 12 feet wide by 12 feet high x 50 feet long cargo bays will be modified to 12 feet x 24 feet x 50 feet and affixed with eight detachable seats, giant size, to better accommodate them in transport. The additional space will be beneficial in other applications as well. We don't know what we will find on Mars; but I believe it will be significant." Winston concluded and turned the podium back to the president.

President Howell stepped to the podium and looked at Winston and then around at the rest of the group. "I agree with those recommendations in consideration of the giants. Also, I've scheduled an appearance before the general assembly of the United Nations. It has become clear to me that this matter is too big to remain an American exclusive. All the nations should be involved in Earth taking its first steps to becoming part of the galactic community. I have had conversations with various heads of state that wish to support it financially and be involved. It's a new day. We have a selection process underway to include a total of 14 representatives, two each from seven other countries."

NASA Headquarters

Winston Stone instructed the group assembled for the posturing of Discovery for the up and coming

Mars Mission. Discovery's engineering staff was to so configure the Land of the Giants, Deck 4, to allow embarking and disembarking without the aid of lifts or gangways. No such conveniences would be waiting on the red planet. Further, the mothership would have to accommodate a larger compliment for a longer period of time. And, it was pointed out by Mentar, that it just might be the case of Discovery finding survivors on Mars as well.

Work began immediately on an elevator and stairs, allowing access from Deck 4 to the massive main ramp of the mother ship. Food storage and supply space was greatly increased as well as stored oxygen and air scrubbing supplies. Guppy 1 and 2 were flown to Chicago for the alteration to the cargo bays. Discovery would be ready within a matter of weeks.

The process of crew selection began with the major nations around the globe. The fact that the selection process involved matters concerning the future of Earth and its inhabitants tended to help melt away many of the petty stumbling blocks that had always complicated agreements between different nations. All must speak English. All must have the necessary training to be able to contribute to the Mission.

Two of the Counselors were included in the ships Manifest. Mentar, the recognized leader of the giant population, and Meta, a female Counselor. Each of those picked an assistant; Mentar picked Kronos, a male, and Meta picked Mayan, a female for her assistant. The two Counselors collectively picked the sixteen students whose parents had retired and relocated to Mars shortly before the disaster. They were eleven males and five females. These students wanted to see if they could find their parents and hopefully, a relic to cherish. Some of them had mentioned hope for their parents but Mentar and Meta had a session with each of them and a serious exchange about reality. However, they too wished for a miracle. He informed Marvin of the sixteen student's special interest in the Mission and their special hope for a miracle, then added that he and Meta had counseled them about reality. Marvin had voiced: "They can hope for a miracle; they themselves are."

The other two Counselors, Brock and Mingee, would remain on Earth to maintain order among the giants. They noted and informed the rest of the giant population that Discovery's refitting also included radio communication equipment installed on Deck 4; land of the giants, and its counterpart at Giant City, Kansas. They would be receiving messages from their friends during the Mars Mission. A link that would be the avenue of Mentar's first sewing of seeds of their ancient home among the stars.

Mentar contacted the president's liaison and requested a refresher course in English for the giant community immediately upon learning of the Mars Mission being planned. Although the course had been taught during their therapy sessions soon after arrival on Earth, and his kind had mastered the basics very well, Mentar felt it critical that they understand all English utterances being spoken to them. This was a trying time for his people and communication was all important with those that held their future in their hands.

DAN HOLT

Chapter 2

LIAISON

The White House

"Pregnant!!"   President Howell exclaimed. "What do you mean, pregnant?!"

"Pregnant, Sir," Dwight Cummins, special liaison to the giants said, "one of the giants is pregnant."

Walter Howell rolled his chair back and tossed his pen onto his desk. "Please tell me that it wasn't one of our teenagers."

"No, Sir," Dwight said, struggling to keep a straight face, "it was one of the giants. A young man named Aledo. The girl is called Milan."

President Howell paused a few moments. "Another bombshell. Why, me?"

"Because you were there, Sir, and you did what America always does; you extended a helping hand. The couple is quite delighted about it. They are going to have the first Earth baby."

The president picked up his pen and nodded. "Okay, let's get some of these giants in medical school. They are supposed to be smart. How big are their babies when they are born?"

"Between five and six feet long."

"Good Lord. What is their gestation period?"

"Twenty-One months, Sir."

"Okay, check with the Counselors and have them pick four of the students and we'll get them in medical school right away."

"Yes, Sir."

The news spread like wildfire around the planet. The White House, Congress, and multiple news agencies were barraged with phone calls and letters. Some claiming deceit on the part of the giants of trying to have Anchor babies and claim Earth. Others were submitting names for the baby. One letter cruelly suggested: Godzilla.

Chapter 3

LAUNCH

Discovery, now complete, sat on its launch pad at Aurora, Illinois. Multiple technicians were going over the systems and the equipment that had been added to the ship. Six of the thirty Rotor Pods were humming, putting Discovery on internal power. Six additional backup Rotor Pods were mounted on motorized trollies and jockeyed on board to join the three backups already stored in the tool room. Thirty-four million miles is a long way from home.

The general inspection would last for days.

NASA Conference Room, Houston.

Colonel Andrews looked at the memo, listing the foreign guests that would be boarding Discovery. It read:

Russia—Colonel Jakov Ivanski, Moscow and Alexia Mulinkov, Gagarin

China—Cheng Yong, Beijing and De Liang, Shanghai

India—Abhay Bengali, Calcutta and K C Thomas, Mumbai

Japan—Akio Aihara, Toyko and Namiko Abe, Osaka

The EU—Darren Page, London and Bernard Derek, Berlin

Australia—Ethan Thomas, Sydney and William Hogan, Perth

Africa—Ammon Tacitus and Kago Tebogo, South Africa

Colonel Ivanski, Russian Air Force Officer and Cosmonaut, approached Colonel Andrews.

"Colonel Andrews," Ivanski said and extended his hand. Marvin locked eyes with him and nodded, then took his hand and shook it.

"I envy you, Colonel," Ivanski said. "You bet everything on that first Mission to the Moon. Maybe, something I would do."

"We didn't think about the risk, Colonel; we had to know," Marvin responded.

Ivanski nodded and smiled. "Lucky for the giants."

"Yeah, I guess it was," Marvin said. "Colonel, glad to have you aboard. When we get to Mars, we may find that we've only scratched the surface on this matter."

"I'm sure of it, Colonel, sure of it."

Colonel Andrews and his bridge crew; Frank Gordon, Douglas Hastings, Roger Stahls, Daniel Stubblefield, and David Henson, were introduced to the players from around the globe that were invited on the Mars Mission. It would be a unilateral endeavor with the United States the authority on determining the final course of action once the sum and substance of the giant's presence in the Solar System was known.

Marvin and crew found it exhilarating that spirits were high, the different peoples blending well, and the giants, to be picked up prior to launch at their temporary location, seeming to be just part of the team. Congress, in their appropriations for the alterations to Discovery and the two guppies, had funded twenty-four additional pressure suits for the giants joining the crew for the Mars Mission. These suits were radio-linked to the fleet. When this decision was made, after much debate, it was decided to change all pressure suits to radio linking. Tethered arrangements were available as well for particularly dangerous excursions.

Late evening - The Cosmos Club - Houston

Colonel Andrews, his bridge crew, Karen and Jean, the pilots of the six shuttles and two guppies, and the two Russian guests sat around a table at the popular Cosmos Club. The Club, organized when President Dwight David Eisenhower breathed life into the National Aeronautics and Space Administration in 1958, grew in popularity and became the gathering place of many who served at NASA.

As the evening wore on Alexia sought out and addressed Maggie Bowden, pilot of Guppy 2. "I saw you on the television and the NASA animation of the rescue of the Guppy 1 on the Moon."

Maggie nodded.

Alexia continued: "Very clever maneuver, Ms. Bowden."

"Call me Maggie, and thank you, we were fortunate that it turned out well."

"Were you rewarded with some of that American money?"

"No," Maggie said, then grinned, "I got a marriage proposal."

"But you are already married."

"I haven't given him an answer."

Alexia grinned. "I like you Americans."

Marvin glanced around the table and located Daniel. "How long will it take us to get to Mars?" Daniel looked up from his cream of potato soup appetizer, swallowed, then cleared his throat. "Thirty-four and a half hours provided we launch in about six weeks; the time when Mars is closest to Earth. The launch window using rocketry is about 23 days. However, we have a much larger window than that with the advent of Magnetic Inertial Propulsion. Obviously, the best time to launch is at the closest approach."

"Discovery is ready," Dave joined. "Her sensors have been set at maximum since we are venturing farther into space. As we increase our relative speed it's possible that something small might get close enough, before it's picked up by the AVS Avoidance System, to penetrate Discovery. NASA is sharp. They think of those things. They developed a GOOPGUN, that seals the hole if we are hit by a meteorite. The so called GOOPGUN is neat. It fires a wafer of material with compressed air into a breach and seals it instantly. The maintenance guys rode NASA's special plane, the vomit comet, several times down through the clouds on Earth practicing sealing holes in various structures to know how to handle it, even under duress."

Six weeks later

Discovery's two guppies descended into a cordoned off area just outside the construction site and near the temporary tent city of the giants west of Wichita, Kansas. The cargo doors were opened to pick up the sixteen souls to be part of the Mars Mission; eight on each ship. The giants shut down their construction work to attend a send-off ceremony of the hand-picked representatives of Giant City, Kansas. As the Mission members entered the guppies, cheers and well-wishes were heard throughout the attending crowd of giants, many of them in English. The 16 were flown to Discovery and escorted to Deck 4. Guppy 1 returned to the plains of Kansas and picked up the two counselors and their chosen assistants.

Departure

Discovery rose from the launch pad fully laden with supplies and bearing 242 members of the ship's company. 208 of Discovery's assigned compliment plus 20 giants and 14 representatives from around the globe. The Mars Mission was underway.

Following the cautionary traversing of the first 25,000 miles, with all personnel strapped in their seats, Discovery was clear of the satellite belts and orbiting debris field of Earth and sailing on along a telemetry flight path to the Red Planet. Colonel Andrews called a ship-wide conference for the formal introductions of the 14 guests from around the world that were invited to join the Mission. The conference would be broadcast throughout the ship, with a visual in the three lounges and video equipped work stations. The ship's communications and records department would make the introductions. Michael Sheridan's son, Robert W. Sheridan, fresh out of San Jose State, finishing with a major in Journalism, would do the honors. Michael Sheridan, a member of the original ground crew for the groundbreaking Research One, beamed with pride when his son, Robert, was picked to head up the Communication and Records Department of Discovery. The bridge crew took only seconds to make the decision.

The 14 guest voyagers filed into the conference room and seated themselves behind a curved table. Each was asked to stand when introduced and their area of study explained.

Robert Sheridan began. "Attention all personnel, Colonel Andrews, commanding Discovery, has requested that we, Ship's Records, formally introduce to you the 14 guests from around the world that have been invited to join us on this Mission to Mars. Our guests are English speaking and skilled individuals, one and all.

"**From Russia**: Colonel Jakov Ivanski, Moscow and Alexia Mulinkov, Gagarin.

Colonel Ivanski is an Air Force Pilot and Cosmonaut. He has flown two space missions and was a participant in a confinement test; a psychological study, where he was tethered to a fellow Cosmonaut for a period of eight months. Their tether allowed no more than six feet separation from each other. They successfully completed the test to determine if forced close quarters, with the same individual, for extended periods of time, would be a debilitating problem.

Alexia is a scientist from Gagarin; the Russian city named after Yuri Gagarin, Russia's first Cosmonaut to orbit the Earth. Her field of study is extended space flight.

"From China: Cheng Yong, Beijing and De Liang, Shanghai.

Cheng is an astronaut-in-training for the space program of the Peoples Republic of China, known as China National Space Administration.

De is an electronics expert with the National Space Administration.

"From India: Abhay Bengali, Calcutta and K C Thomas, Mumbai.

Abhay is an anthropologist and a linguist.

K. C., no first name, just the initials, is a climatologist. Just a note of interest: K. C. is Mr. Thomas' address as well as his name. K Street, C Dwelling in the experimental neighborhood in which he lives.

"From Japan: Akio Aihara, Tokyo and Namiko Abe, Osaka.

Akio and Namiko both are researchers in Artificial Intelligence.

"From the European Union: Darren Page, London and Bernard Derek, Berlin.

Darren is a mechanical engineer and metallurgist.

Bernard is also a computer programmer in A.I. research.

"From Australia: Ethan Thomas, Sydney and William Hogan, Perth.

Ethan, one of Australia's favorite sons, is a scientist in radio astronomy and SETI research. He was involved, at the age of 19, in the receiving of the signals from the Moon during Apollo 11's broadcast, and transmitting them on to Houston.

William is a scientist involved in extensive research on meteorites, making use of Australia's giant *catcher's mitt*; the outback.

"From Africa: Ammon Tacitus and Kago Tebogo, both, South Africa.

Ammon, an organizer with administrative training, is working on solidifying a viable space program on the African continent, exhaustively petitioning all the states to get involved in The South African National Space Agency. He campaigned extensively to be included on Discovery's journey.

Kago is a Planner in the organization of the African Space Agency.

That concludes our formal introductions. Each of these guests has expressed a desire to speak to each of you sometime during Discovery's Mission. Thank you for your attention."

As the earth receded farther and farther into the distance, members of the crew ventured to the windshield of Discovery, the section on either side of the bridge's control area, and checked on that special point of light—Earth. Its recession among the stars seemed to unify the peoples of the Mission. The representatives of the various governments, in each of the lounges, began to spontaneously interact, forming an away-from-home bond with their fellow travelers. Groups, like the Chinese, the European representatives, and the Australians went to visit with the giants as a group; wanting to know more about who they are and where they came from.

Many groups, made up of all the different nations, made similar gestures of camaraderie with the giants and, strangely, the size deferential seemed to disappear. With Earth far away and the mission details yet unknown, they seemed to form a bond of a mutual quest. The world ahead on Mars had no players onboard Discovery. All souls aboard were orphans; all looking for answers.

The Starship Discovery sailed on through the Cosmic night. If one could approach and peer through the portholes there would be multiple roundtables of discussion, mouths moving energetically, discussing the incredible adventure. Earth had been thrust into a new reality and its players were savoring every moment.

Chapter 4

THE BULLET

Marvin, Doug, Dave, and Roger, leaving Frank and Daniel at Discovery's helm, went up the stairs to the Land of the Giants, Deck 4, for a conference regarding arrival at the Red Planet. The updated appointments constructed into Deck 4 accommodated the meeting quite well. It was a conference table matching the sizing of Deck 4's occupants on one side and scaled down seven times on the other side with a raised platform for an eye level arrangement,

"Mentar and Meta," Marvin began, "we need to know the best place to look for the lab, the retirement community, and whatever else might be on Mars. Any information you may have; perhaps tidbits you've heard. Anything could help. Obviously it's all underground like it was on the Moon. Our satellites have photographed Mars for years and have seen nothing conclusive. Granted, there's the controversy of the, so called, *face* on Mars, a hominid-appearing face, and the nearby pyramid-shaped mountains, but they've never been officially recognized. If there's no other information or ideas, we'll start there.

"I think of nothing new, Colonel," Mentar said. "We were not concerned about the activities of the scientists of our culture. Our concern was our group of students completing their first stage of entering adulthood on Solaris 4."

Doug joined in: "I would think that the thing to do is check the Cydonia Region of Mars first. Maybe the face-like covering is over the lab as a simple marker of its location. I read quite a bit on it while I was researching the Apollo Missions. They presented a convincing case of intelligent design. That just might be where it is."

"Well," Marvin said, "it seems strange that our satellites haven't seen any ruins, foundations, or anything conclusive that Mars was ever..."

Suddenly, a loud pinging sound echoed through Discovery. It sounded like a blacksmith's hammer striking his anvil. A klaxon began resounding loudly throughout the ship accompanied by the ship's intercom: *Warning, hull breach, Deck 4. Warning, hull breach, Engine Room. Warning, hull breach, Deck 4. Warning, hull breach, Engine Room.*

Marvin and company jumped to their feet and began searching the ceiling of Deck 4. Soon, they spotted it; a hole about a half inch in diameter, below it, the same size hole went through one of the giant's seats, fortunately unoccupied. Marvin bounded to the stairs and down them. At the foot of the stairs two maintenance men ran past him up the stairs carrying two of the GOOPGUNS. They were taking the stairs two at a time. Marvin ran to the console. Frank, on Marvin's approach, pointed at the rotor pod monitor. One of the pod's status lights were blinking in the red. The power output read **ZERO**. The power percentage readout on the two pods on either side of it had increased 50% each. Dave, arriving right behind Marvin, joined Daniel in running diagnostic programs.

"The breach in the engine room is below that pod," Marvin shouted, pointing at the blinking red light on the readout.

Frank looked at the readout again. "It's rotor pod number 17!"

Marvin nodded. "I'm going to the engine room. Daniel, call medical and find out about injuries."

Marvin ran to the access stairs to the engine room. At the foot of the stairs he looked around. The maintenance team was already there, searching the floor. "It's below pod #17, Marvin shouted." Maintenance quickly located pod #17 and the breach, affixed the GOOPGUN and fired the sealing mixture into the hole. It hardened in seconds and the venting stopped.

"Okay, gentlemen," Marvin said. "Problem solved. Check the path of that meteorite and see where we've been damaged, then go ahead and change out this rotor pod right away. Let's keep Discovery at peak operational status. Let me know if there's any serious problems"

"Yes, Sir," the crew echoed.

Deck 4

The maintenance team, topping the stairs, hurried to the spot of the breach, examined it, then two of the men ran toward the maintenance storage locker for a ladder to reach the fifty-foot ceiling. Mentar glanced at the two men hurrying across the deck, then reached down and laid his hand on the floor in front of one of the men holding the GOOPGUNS, then pointed at the palm of his hand. The maintenance man looked up at his face. He nodded. The maintenance man quickly stepped up onto the palm of the giant's hand. Mentar positioned his other hand circling the maintenance man as a safety bucket, then lifted him up to the ceiling and the rupture. The maintenance man then placed the GUN over the hole and fired the sealant into place. It quickly hardened, sealing the rupture. Mentar put him back on the floor. The maintenance man pointed up at him: "You are now a member of my team."

Mentar nodded then looked around at his colleagues. A couple of them patted him on the back.

Marvin returned to the bridge and canceled the alarms.

"Colonial," Daniel said, "one of the circulation fans on Deck 3 has failed."

"Gentlemen, we just took a bullet. Maintenance will trace the path of that meteorite that went through the ship and check everything for damage. Notify them about that fan."

"Will do, Colonial, everything else is clear according to the computers. Also, we were lucky; no injuries reported."

The half-inch diameter, incredibly dense, projectile sailed on in a new orbit. Having been slowed a few miles-per-second, it would never pass this way again. Its encounter with a space-borne object a million times its size gave it a new adventure. It would spend a quarter-million-years seeking out and taking aim at a lonely star. It would make a suicide plunge into its heart to be melted down, reformed, then with the upcoming nova be launched again to a new destination.

Chicago Linguistics Institute – Earth

Della Clayton, linguist, turned to her three team members. "You agree?"

The three researchers nodded in unison. The older of the three, Evelyn Watson, called out of retirement to have the benefit of her vast experience in ancient languages, spoke conclusively. "It's Nahuatl," she said and paused a moment, then made a note on her write-up: *Pronounced: Nay-Watt-uL*, "It's still spoken in the rural areas of central Mexico by about a million and a half people. The language has borrowed some Spanish words over the centuries, but it's still Nahuatl."

Della paused a moment. "The language of the Aztec Indians. Let's radio Discovery and let Karen know. Prepare a statement that I can read into a radio message."

Discovery – 16,000,000 miles from Earth

Karen, Doug, Jean, Dave, Marvin, Roger, plus Edgar and Joyce; the two linguists that had gained Lunar experience, sat around a table in the aft lounge. They noticed that at several of the tables across the lounge there were groups that included one or two of the guests on Discovery, engaged in very active discussions. Marvin nodded approvingly.

The intercom came alive.

Karen Hastings, you have a message from the Chicago Linguistics Institute; repeat; Karen Hastings, you have a message from the Chicago Linguistics Institute.

Karen glanced around the table. "Let's take this party to my lab."

The party stood and followed Karen.

When everyone was seated Karen keyed the radio. The message began:

Karen: This is Della Clayton. As you know, I and my team have been studying the books discovered in the building outside the lab complex on the Moon. More specifically the building that the reports have designated as "The Library." Since the Mars mission was sanctioned we have been working on the section in the Library dedicated to the planet Mars. We have made some significant discoveries that we feel you should know about since, in a matter of hours, you will be arriving on Mars and will begin exploration of the activities that were underway there.

First: These writings indicate that the giants, their scientists, planned to manufacture mechanical units, mobile units, that would be programmed to service the starship and its crew when in route to the binary star system they call home. There are some descriptions of the physical stature of the robots. They are to be bi-ped, about twelve feet tall, and have 360 degree visual receptors. The arms on the units are to have extra length, reaching almost to the knees, with six fingers and two opposing thumbs on each hand. I can only wonder about their appearance. We could not determine how far along they were on their development so we felt you should know about them and can approach their lab there with caution.

Second: This is puzzling. They were creating a special group of genetic little ones on the Moon and depositing them on the Earth separate from the others. They kept checking on them periodically. Later, when the separate colony began to grow and develop, they came, picked up some of them and took them to Mars. They put them in suspended animation to test their equipment they designed for putting themselves in suspended animation for the journey to the stars! Here's the big surprise; the language they created for them is Nahuatl!!

Good luck.
Della Clayton.

Marvin stepped over to the intercom and keyed the unit: "Akio, Namiko, and Bernard to the Linguistics Lab." Marvin returned to his seat. "A race of robots," he said. "Robots wouldn't be affected by the loss of atmosphere and pressure when the disaster occurred. If they had some of them completed and programmed before the tragedy, they may still be active now. Of course that would be a long shot because their power supply would have had to have lasted thousands of years."

"The lights on the Moon still worked," Dave said.

"Yeah, I know," Marvin responded, "but, they were mechanical in nature and function and were powered by the Sun which didn't quit working at the point of the disaster. It's possible that the robots are still working if their power is replenished by the Sun periodically. That's why I want these A I programmers to know about this. They might pick up on something significant and can alert us."

The A.I. researchers arrived.

Marvin indicated a chair then turned to Karen. "Karen, replay that message for these guys."

Karen restarted the message and it played again. The A.I. specialists listened intently, then, when it finished, asked to hear it again. Karen complied.

"Just wanted to let you know about this development," Marvin said. "With as much time that has passed; at least fifty thousand years, it's likely that they are not functioning now; that is, if they were functioning before the cataclysm. However, we don't know that so you may be able to advise us somewhat if they are active.

The three programmers nodded. "Anything we can do," Bernard stated and the three left the lab.

Marvin turned to Karen; she was doing a search on the lab's language computers. "What about these *little ones* that Della mentioned in that message?"

Karen turned to Marvin and the group. "Nahautl is the language of the Aztec Indians that flourished in Central America. They, the Aztec, the ones in our history, were sacrificing to and always waiting for the return of their god, Quetzalcoatl. They must have thought that the giants were gods.

Apparently the Aztec were cave dwellers at the time of the disaster and after the dust settled, they never saw the giants again."

Marvin added: "So, they began sacrificing, some of it horrendous, to the gods trying to get them to return."

Karen nodded. "There's well over a million people living in central Mexico, in the rural areas, right now, that still speak Nahautl."

"Okay," Marvin surmised, "if we find these Aztec people on Mars in suspended animation, we can awaken them and return them to their own people?"

"There will be a serious gap in lifeways, language usage, and values, but, yes, yes we can."

"I've got a question," Roger said. "Why would the giants want to leave the Solar System. Before they screwed up and caused their home planet, here, to explode, the Solar System was a prize. Four livable planets, technology affording them ease of travel one to the other, fantastic retirement facilities, and challenges to grow and learn; everything that makes life great."

"Professor Liggins summed that up rather neatly," Karen said, "in his speech before the *Meeting of the Minds Conference*. This is not their home. The giants simply want to go home."

"It appears that they dedicated all of their society's resources toward that effort," Jean added.

"It now seems that, maybe, some of those efforts had turned dark," Marvin said quietly.

"Twenty minutes until Zero-G transfer to the deceleration phase," was announced throughout Discovery.

Chapter 5

ARRIVAL

A robot, receiving a signal from its central energy storage capacitor assembly, began its climb to the pinnacle of the interior of the pyramid. Upon reaching the topmost platform, it moved into its designated cubicle, slid the shutter open exposing the raw energy of the Sun, then focused on the bright disc. When the Sun's energetic rays were centered on its internal grid, it locked on and began automatically tracking the sun across the sky. It would maintain its lock until its system was fully recharged.

Of its countless recharging cycles, this time, a new object entered its field of view. The object was decelerating. Unable to wonder, unable to care, there was no reaction at all.

Mars Orbit

"Okay," Daniel said, "telemetry's disengaged."

"What's that?" Dave said, pointing at the radar screen.

"Phobos, the inner moon of Mars," Daniel replied, "about to pass over us. She's about 2000 miles higher above the planet than Discovery. We are 1800 miles above the surface of Mars."

Colonel Andrews keyed the intercom. "Ship's company, we have arrived. Communications, log the time and notify Earth. As soon as a ship-wide review is complete, we'll descend to the surface."

Momentarily, Discovery was cleared to land and descended to the surface of the red planet. Marvin set the ship's altitude at a cautionary *flying at ground level*. The twenty-two-mile-high extinct volcano, Olympus Mons, two miles away, loomed through the porthole. Discovery's shadow, cast by the late evening sun, almost reached her base. Many made their way across Discovery to view the distant sun. It's smallness and relative dim appearance seemed to trigger a false sense of shivering coolness.

The Sun was setting on the newly established city of Discovery, Mars; the first metropolis that had flourished in many thousands of years. A calm settled on the ship. This was the second celestial body that Discovery had graced other than Earth, her home. The crewmembers grouped in the lounges and the cafeteria for an evening meal and camaraderie. All were filled with awe, caution, and wonder. As the minutes and hours ticked by they all pillowed their heads for their first Martian night.

Marvin sat in his quarters, at his desk, reviewing the manifest of Discovery, especially the guests from the various other countries. He wanted to involve them in this Mission of investigation. He settled on assigning them shuttles for the initial search through the complex. He would take the lead in Shuttle One with three experienced crewmembers and two of the guests. Guppy 1 would follow with Mentar, Kronos, Meta, and Mayan on board. The other three shuttles would put four each of the guests with the pilot and navigator. That would give all fourteen of them a true sense of involvement.

He made notes on his clipboard:

Shuttle One: Marvin, Doug, Dave, Roger, and Russian Team—Ivan and Alexia.

Shuttle Two: Chinese and Japanese Teams—Cheng, De, Akio, and Namiko.

Shuttle Three: Indian and African Teams—Abhay, K C, Ammon, and Kago.

Shuttle Four: EU and Australian Teams—Darren, Bernard, Ethan, and William.

Dusk

Mentar leaned his seat back, waiting for the Sun to drop below the Martian horizon and darkness to come. His mind, waiting for night, began to review the disturbing developments of which he had just learned. The activities of the scientists, the self-appointed leaders of his society, were troublesome. He had discussed it with Meta. She also had misgivings about some of the past activities of Solaris 4's government. The manipulation of life on Earth, the genetic combinations that had resulted in the advent of the *Little Ones* had always felt uncomfortable for Mentar. He was born into a society where that practice had been established for a very long time. Now, it was becoming clear that change was in order. Also, *now* was the perfect time to affect such sweeping reform. The students were not yet indoctrinated into the social order that had been in place so long ago. When Discovery was back home on Earth he would discuss this with Brock and Mingee as well.

The sixteen students, plus Meta, the Counselor, along with Kronos, and Mayan were venturing port hole to port hole studying the desolate Martian landscape outside. The scene was a stark reminder of a previous reality; the closing of the curtain on their tenure on the Moon. Utterly destroyed. Here, the feelings of helplessness played through the psyche again. The ever-lengthening shadows seemed a timed closure.

Mentar turned on the radio console. The students gathered around the terminal. Mentar, reminding the students that there would be a ten-minute delay from transmit to receive during the radio contact with Earth, keyed the link to Giant City, Kansas.

"Brock, Mingee, come in please."

The students engaged in small talk, watching the clock...

"Mentar, we've been waiting!"

The response of the voices from Earth was mesmerizing...

"We just landed; the Sun is just going down. We'll be spending the night here, and will then proceed to locate the lab in the morning."

"It's noon here on Earth. How's it going so far?"

"We were hit by a meteorite but the rupture was fixed." From the students behind Mentar, in raised voices to be heard over the radio, came: "Mentar helped the little ones seal the hole in the ship. He saved the ship." A buzz passed through the gathering group of the students as they learned that Mentar was calling from Mars.

"Aledo, Mentar said, "How's Milan doing?"

"Just fine," Aledo said. *"The little ones brought one of their ice cream trucks for her. She's almost got it empty already."*

Mentar chuckled, wished her the best, then described the surface of Mars that was visible from the initial landing site. Also he reassured the group on Earth that an important attempt to locate some of their own would be a part of the venture. The commander of the ship felt it important for the well-being of all concerned.

Mentar signed off on the radio with a promise to call again soon.

Giant City, Kansas, was abuzz with the story of Mentar saving the ship and the little ones on their way to Mars. The giants had a hero.

As night crept across Discovery, Mentar's eyes went to the huge window. He would search the fifty-foot diameter transparent acrylic viewport in Discovery's topmost hull, looking to the south, hoping to locate Alpha Centauri, the third brightest star in the sky. He had known for a long time that it was where they, his people, had come from. It had not been of any particular significance until he was ordered into an induced sleep along with the students in his charge, then awakened millenniums later to find his home utterly erased. Now, it seemed to matter. There was a deep yearning to know more about it, to go back there, now that there's nothing here that they, his own kind, could call home. Aledo and Milan; their baby will be born in the *land of the Little Ones*. We are losing our identity.

The Little Ones; perhaps they would help....

Dawn – First Day

The Sun began its daily chore of bringing the atmosphere of Mars from bitter cold, up to cold. Its distant influence marked dawn on the red planet as efficiently as ever. The arisen crew of Discovery, filled with curiosity, began the first day. Electricity was in the air.

Marvin keyed the intercom: "Shuttles One through Four, launch and fly north, south, east, and west, respectively. Fly two miles, scouting the area and reporting the results, then return to the ship. Shuttles Five and Six, overfly the Cydonia Region and report. Guppies 1 and 2, you're on standby."

Shuttles One through Four flew their assignments, reporting nothing but desolate Martian countryside, covered mostly by the famous reddish tinted soil that was evident over the entire planet. Shuttles Five and Six were nearing the Cydonia Region several hundred miles away. As they approached the target area, their radio contact with Discovery went dark. As per instructions from the communications department of the mother ship, Shuttle Six rose to 2000 feet altitude, reestablished line-of-sight radio communications with the mother ship, and then set up a relay for Shuttle Five.

Over Cydonia - Mars

Melissa Ryan, pilot of Shuttle Five, began circling over Cydonia. She keyed the radio. "Discovery, this is Shuttle Five, we are over the Cydonia Region. Colonel, this face-like structure is enormous. It's well over a mile from top to bottom and almost a mile side to side. There is lots of sand all over the place. A mile or so from the face are several irregular pyramid shapes; rather large pyramids. They are located on one side of the face. Then, below the face there's more of them.

Also, beyond the pyramids there are pipes or tubes; actually, they look like giant worms, half buried in the surface, going off into the distance.

K. C. Thomas keyed the intercom: "Colonel, this is K. C. Thomas, Mumbai, those pipes or tubes are lava tubes. I studied the Martian surface at length. In the early history, when she was volcanically active, those tubes were formed as lava flowed freely on the planet."

"Thank you Mr. Thomas. Shuttle Five, acknowledge?"

"Colonel!", Melissa shouted into the shuttles radio, "there are tracks here! We followed a tube away from the Cydonia area and we came to a break in it. Sir, there are tracks in the sand. Someone has been walking inside this tube!"

A stir spread through Discovery. Marvin keyed the radio. "Shuttle Five and Six, return to Discovery, immediately."

"Yes, Sir, on our way."

Onboard Discovery

With all the shuttles recalled and moored in Discovery, Colonel Andrews called a planning meeting in the main conference room: "Okay, we know that there's activity at Cydonia. Let's move Discovery to the region, park over the face at 500 feet for a command center, then began our investigation. Discovery will have the safety of the sky."

Liftoff

Discovery rose from the surface, steered to the right, and soon entered the majestic Valles Marineris. She flew along the canyon a thousand feet from the north wall. As the miles rolled by the canyon wall seemed to ripple far and close relative to Discovery. Dozens of sets of eyes, through the portholes and on the monitors, searched for anything artificial; anything resembling the telltale artifacts found on the moon. The beauty of the canyon's sheer cliffs was mesmerizing.

In just over three hours the marker, a computer generated line in the sand that extended through the Cydonia Region, was reached and Discovery rose above the wall of the deep trench in the Martian surface. She rotated north and began to cruise toward the objective. The landscape was relatively flat for some few miles. There was a noticeable absence of ruins, at least the foundations, that were expected to be there. A mystery that needed an answer. Marvin stopped Discovery and ordered four of the shuttles out to escort Discovery and do close inspections, with their size advantage, when needed. When they were staffed and launched, he resumed Discovery's flight to the Cydonia Region.

Up ahead, there appeared samples of the *"giant worms,"* as described by Shuttle Six. There were broken places in the tubes where the roof and walls were missing for fifty to a hundred feet, then the tube would resume.

Discovery slowed and followed a larger lava tube that ran virtually due-north. There was another break in the tube up ahead. It looked like about a hundred feet of the tube's roof was gone. Marvin slowed Discovery and studied the break for tracks. As the fleet got closer it became clear that there was a trail that came out of the tube, then re-entered it at the other side of the gap. Shuttles One and Two descended down to a few feet above the tube for a closer look. "Colonel," Shuttle One reported. There are tracks alright; they're about twice the size of human footprints."

"That would be about right," Marvin noted, "according to Della's report."

Suddenly, two human shaped forms, without pressure suits, emerged from the tube and walked right between the two shuttles, carrying a block-shaped object ten-by-ten by fifty-feet long. One of the machines was on each end of the object and the two were walking in lock-step. The robots completely ignored the shuttles. They proceeded on into the tube again and disappeared. Shuttle One descended down for a visual inside the tube. The crew saw the robots marching on and disappearing around a curve. Jackson glanced at the rear view monitor then rotated the ship one hundred and eighty degrees and checked to see if there were more coming in the tube. It was empty.

"Colonel," Jackson said, "the tube is about thirty feet in diameter. The shuttle will fit, but it would be tight. Shall we follow them?"

Marvin, with Discovery at station-keeping hover, responded: "Not at this time; that tube is very old and degraded. Perhaps later we will try to traverse the tube with two of the ships. Right now, let's do some information-gathering. Shuttles One and Two, back-trace this lava tube and see where it goes. Shuttles three and four, stay in formation with Discovery while we continue to follow this tube to its and the robots' destination. Shuttles five and six, and Guppies 1 and 2, stand at the ready."

Marvin picked up his clipboard, turned a couple of pages, then scanned down the list of invited guests. He keyed the intercom. "Akio Aihara, Namiko Abe, and Bernard Derek to the Bridge."

Shuttles One and Two began tracing the path of the lava tube back to its origin. Shuttles Three and Four, holding their position on either side of Discovery's windshield, paced the Mothership in view of her Bridge Crew.

Daniel, staring through the windshield following the path of the lava tube, glancing around from time to time, then back to the lava tube, said to no one in particular: "Why haven't our satellites gotten pictures of these guys?"

Doug glanced at him. "It would be rare. They would have to be focused on this narrow area, at the right time, and then if it did happen, it would probably be dismissed as rocks or an outcropping or a sand dune."

Marvin eased the stick forward and followed the lava tube ahead. It meandered through the Martian countryside. In places it was completely covered with the red Martian dust, compliments of the planet-wide dust storms. It was soon obvious that the tube would go to the Cydonia region. Maybe some of what the conspiracy theorist claimed; that the tube-like structures were transportation conduits, had credence. Obviously those mechanical units, as Della Clayton had referred to them, were using them for some purpose.

"Shuttle One, come in," Marvin said into the radio.

"Shuttle One," J.D. responded.

"Anything?"

"Not yet, Sir. We are progressing very slowly. We've come to an area where the tube goes underground or is completely covered with dust for several hundred feet. We are having to re-acquire."

"Understood. Let us know as soon as you know something."

"Yes, Sir."

Akio, Namiko, and Bernard, Artificial Intelligence researchers, responded to the Bridge.

"Were you gentlemen monitoring when the robots appeared briefly?"

"Yes, Colonel," they responded simultaneously.

"What can you tell me from the brief visual we just had?"

"We were just discussing that, Colonel," Akio said. "One; they were walking in lock-step and therefore taking the same length of stride. That indicates that they are communicating with each other constantly; probably a constant data stream each to the other. Two; according to your researcher at the Chicago Linguistics Institute, they have 360 degree visual receptors. Yet, they ignored the two shuttles and Discovery completely. That indicates that they have no programming concerning anything outside their assigned task; whatever that might be."

Namiko joined in: "From what we've seen. It appears that they have no A.I. processors. They just run programs and those programs determine their physical actions." Namiko paused a moment then added: "Sir, a word of caution. From what we've learned about the scientists of Solaris 4, there could be more of them, that look the same, that have much more sophisticated programming."

Bernard Derek joined in: "Let me add that interacting programs; i.e., teamwork as we just saw, is a good platform for the installation of A.I. programming. And, Sir, since some of the robots are supposed to be created to fly their starship, it is likely that some of the robots will have A.I. programming. They will actually be Automatons."

"Automatons?" Roger queried.

Bernard nodded. "Capable of making decisions with regard to what's happening around them and then acting on those decisions to achieve whatever directive has been given them. In this case, the directive would be direct their ship to the Alpha

Centauri System. If anything got in the way of that directive they would address the problem based on their programming, however extensive it was. If they saw no solution, they would wake up the Captain of the ship. A note; since they, at this point, did not have their propulsion system worked out, they may not have active Automatons as yet."

"If they have already developed Automatons, would they have a different appearance?" Marvin asked.

"Not necessarily, however, I believe they would, simply because their creators would want to identify them at a glance. If it was me and they had A.I. programming, I would make them very noticeable."

"Thank you, gentlemen," Marvin said. "Keep me informed on everything you see as we go forward."

"Yes, Sir." The three experts said, then two of them bowed and one nodded and the three left the Bridge.

Marvin glanced at Shuttle Three and Four, then eased the stick forward and resume toward the Cydonia Region. Far in the distance he could see the upper half of the hominid-face-shaped mountain. It spanned over a mile on a north-south line. The lava tube transport-way meandered from time to time, then resumed it northerly direction. The radio broke the silence. "Colonel, this is Shuttle One."

Marvin brought Discovery to a station-keeping hover. "Go ahead."

"Sir, we are at the end of the lava tube. It ends at the wall of an enormous mound. We ascended to five thousand feet to have a look at it from the top and it looks like just another mountain. However, it's very wide for its height. Three or four miles across."

"Is it hollow?"

"Can't tell. We can't see any access or opening from here. There may be somewhere around the base."

"Okay," Marvin said. "Return to the ship and fly escort. We'll investigate that mound later. Discovery will hold until you arrive."

"On our way."

Discovery's linguistics lab

Karen keyed the radio: *"Message to Chicago Linguistics Institute, Attention Della Clayton. Message from: Karen Hastings, Discovery. I need a program transmitted to me. English to Nahuatl—Nahuatl to English. I'll upload it to a mobile translator here in case we actually contact one of the Little Ones still alive. I need that right away. Let me know the time-frame and I'll ready my equipment here. End of message."*

Twenty-two minutes later the radio came alive with the response: *"Yes, it will take about two hours to isolate and integrate the two languages. I'll transmit it to you when we have it ready. End of message."*

Karen leaned back in her chair, paused a moment, then leaned forward again and keyed the intercom. "Colonel, I have a language program being assembled and transmitted to me from the Chicago Institute. It will enable us to talk to the Little Ones if and when we find them. It works with the Nahuatl language to English and vice versa. It will be ready and here in about three hours."

"Understood, Karen, good thinking."

The Bridge

Marvin saw the two shuttles appear on either side of Discovery. He eased the mother ship forward with the four shuttles escorting. The mountain ahead grew larger. He wondered why the giants would choose to copy the face of the great apes of planet

Earth. Was it because their DNA was compatible with the giants themselves, making the hominids a prize *find*? Did the giants come to the Solar System to experiment with life on Earth? Or, after taming Solaris 4, did their experimentation with life on Earth lead to the discovery of compatible animals and then the business of manipulation gradually become part of their culture?

Marvin flew Discovery directly over the face. When he reached the center of the enormous construct, he held, then parked the ship at 500 feet and set Discovery's controls to hover stationary as a base of operations. With the ship *anchored* Marvin sent out two shuttles to circumnavigate the base of the enormous face and check for access doorways that would allow entrance of the shuttles and guppies.

Discovery's Linguistics Lab

Karen's radio came alive, noting an incoming transmission, then began copying a computer program. When it finished, Karen copied it to her mobile translator and then stored it in archives. She notified the Bridge that the language translation program was now on board and available.

The Bridge

"Colonel, this is Shuttle One," came from the radio.

"Go ahead," Marvin responded.

"Sir, we are about the middle of the complex. There's a doorway here. It appears to be the same dimensions as the tunnel on the moon. Also, there are no tracks going in and out. No wheel tracks or footprints. There are sand drifts at the left end of the doorway about four feet deep. Nothing's used this doorway for a very long time."

"Can you see inside?"

"Very little; it's very dimly lighted, or seems to be with it being so bright out here."

"Understood. Do not enter, yet. Continue the survey of the full perimeter."

"Will do."

Shuttle Two headed for the opposite side of the face. She flew directly over one of the eyes of the hominid-imaged mountain. Lucas radioed Discovery:

"Colonel, on our way to the other side of the face we flew over one of the eyes. The pupil looks like a landing pad. It's recessed down into the face about fifty or sixty feet."

"How big?"

"It's about fifty feet across. Big enough for a shuttle, but, probably too small for a Guppy."

"Okay, go ahead and check out the rest of the perimeter of the face."

"Yes, Sir."

The shuttles completed the survey of the exterior of structure then reported back to Discovery. Marvin, noting the late evening shadows of the surrounding pyramid-shaped mountains, ordered the ships in for the day. A very eventful first day would spark discussion for hours. Tomorrow they would enter the lab and know its secrets.

Deck 4

Mentar keyed the radio to reach Giant City, Earth. The waiting giants answered with eagerness for an update. Mentar filled them in on the day's activities and a note that tomorrow they would begin the investigation and then soon after, the search for their own. The brief exchanges lasted over two hours with the agonizing time delays as the earthbound giants lived the event through Mentar's eyes. Then the link was broken and each returned to their thoughts.

Mentar gazed at length at the bright star framed in the transparent circle of Discovery's upper hull. The lights were low and most of the 16 students on board were gazing at the stars or talking among themselves. The voice of Kronos invaded his thoughts: "Mentar, what's going to happen to us?"

Deck 4 became quiet. The students gathered around Mentar. He paused for a long moment then pointed at the circle of stars visible through the port hole. All eyes on Deck 4 went to the viewing window. "Kronos, you see that star, that one, the brightest in the window?"

"Yes."

"That's your home. That's where you belong. The world with two Suns. We are going there."

Kronos turned and looked at Mentar. "How?"

"The little ones can build a ship that will take us there. I must figure out how to get them to do it."

Mentar turned toward the group of giants; his own. "One day we will get home. It will take some time to prepare, perhaps several years, but we will get home. Right now, we must focus on what we are doing here. We will need this equipment, the programming, and much of what's been prepared here. We have much to do."

DAN HOLT

Chapter 6

THE FACE

With the face situated on a north/south line, an identical door opening was located on the four points of the compass. All were 300 feet wide and 70 feet high.

Marvin keyed the intercom: "All shuttle crews, all guppy crews, and all guest teams, report to the main deck."

While the parties were gathering, he went up the stairs for a brief meeting with Mentar. "I want you and Kronos to accompany us inside. I want you're input on what we find in there."

Mentar nodded. "We will be glad to help, Colonel."

Marvin noticed that Mentar's voice was laced with concern. A bit of a red flag for Discovery's commander. Marvin paused just briefly, then nodded. "Put on your pressure suits, minus the helmets." Marvin went back down the stairs.

"Okay," Marvin addressed the conference, "we know of two robots that are now active. They, apparently, are tending something. There may be more of them; more of them that could be more sophisticated. J.D., ready Guppy 1, Mentar and Kronos are accompanying us inside."

Marvin announced the crew that would be boarding shuttles Two, Three, and Four. Colonel Ivanski and his associate, Alexia were informed to board Shuttle One. Shuttle's Five and Six plus Guppy 2 were put on standby.

Shuttlecraft One entered the open doorway of the megastructure, followed by Guppy 1, then shuttles Two, Three, and Four. Marvin looked toward the ceiling. "There are multiple holes in the ceiling from the meteorites penetrating it over the centuries. Dust has invaded and covered everything." He surveyed the ceiling at length then looked out across the mile square enclosure. "This lab is different. I don't see evidence of genetic work here. This facility must be dedicated just to the development of robots. There's lighting all across the ceiling and the pyramid-shaped light-gathering equipment like we saw on the Moon, but that appears to be all."

Doug, scanning the floor, said, "There are multiple stations scattered across the floor that look like radios or computers arranged in a semicircle layout. Maybe they are programming stations or uploading stations."

Marvin studied one of them. "We'll have Guppy Two detach one of those stations and take it to Discovery to return to Earth for study."

"Where are the giants?" Roger said from Shuttle Two. "We haven't seen any bodies of the giants, no tracks on the floor, or anything to indicate that people were working here when the things went bad for them."

Marvin added, "Over thousands of years, dust would gradually cover all the evidence of tracks, however, the bodies of the giants would be visible. Mars, because of its orbit, was closer to Solaris 4 than Earth when both were on the close approach side of their orbits. It would have been first to suffer the wrath of the explosion. Since Earth survived, it's likely that it was on the other side of the Sun when it happened."

J.D. added: "If they had ships available, they would board them and fly out of the maelstrom to survive, even with no particular place to go."

"Colonel," Mentar said in his low-pitched voice, bringing silence in all five ships and throughout Discovery, "they may have had a place to go. They may have fled to the ancient starship that they were in the process of restoring to service. No one knows how far along they were with it. It is almost half the diameter of your moon. They could have had it far enough along to support them, at least a few of them, for a period of time."

That's the one you've mentioned before; the one that's in orbit around Saturn?"

"Yes. It has become apparent that they were working on the sleeping units, both for them and for some of the Little Ones and working on tending machines, the robots, to use during the return flight to home. They were also working on a power supply to drive the ship and we know what happened there. The original star drive in the ancient ship could not be restored to service. I would like to talk to your president about that."

There was silence for several moments. Then Marvin spoke. "I believe I can get you an appointment."

Frank observed, "Why wouldn't the giants, that left here and went to the ship for a time, simply fly back to Earth after the dust settled and live there?"

"They probably did," Doug said. "Maybe there simply wasn't enough of them to propagate the race; perhaps only a couple dozen or so. And, they simply died out."

At Marvin's direction, J.D. set a course north toward the *forehead* of the building. Soon they came to cordoned-off areas, each having different parts of robot bodies, limbs, servos, electronic processors, and various sized capacitors designed to store electric power. They saw a robot head lying on a bench with a chair positioned next to it. There were tools lying beside the head, one square-shaped tube about an inch on a side and twenty inches long with a handle on it was leaning up against the head. It appeared to have been abandoned in process, as if the technician was in a serious hurry. The head had a black screen-like window circling it just above the nose. The window was about an inch bottom to top and was recessed into the cranium about a half-inch.

"Talk about eyes in the back of your head," Doug commented, "look at that."

There were dozens of work stations with different parts of the anatomy of a mechanical man-shaped unit. Marvin looked south across the mile-long room. "Let's fly to the other end of the lab."

The Armada flew into the south end of the lab, into the narrowing *chin* of the face-like structure. As they closed on the end-most parts of the lab, stacks of containers came into view. They looked like miniature versions of the glass crates in which the giants on the moon were found. They were 2 x 4 x 8 feet; human-sized.

"I've got a feeling about what we are going to find.   Remember Della's communication?   Let's descend to the floor level and locate access to what's bound to be underground."

Chapter 7

THE TUNNEL

The three ships began a systematic search of the floor of the ancient building, making their way around the work stations, electronic equipment, and unknown machinery. Half an hour later the announcement came from Shuttle Two: "We found it, it's about dead center in the building. The entrance is covered by a Quonset Hut. There's a shaft about a hundred feet square going into the floor. There are stairs on one side of it that zig zag downward. It's dark down there.

Shuttle One, hovering over the entrance shaft, began its descent down into the underground tunnel. About a hundred feet down the ship passed through a projected beam of light. The vertical shaft and tunnels below were bathed in light, one leading toward the pyramid complex to the west, and the other on the opposite side of the vertical shaft, leading east. Marvin stopped the ship and held. "Looks like they were using the same Solar-Mechanical lighting system here also."

Darren Page, mechanical engineer from London, stared into the light-filled Quonset Hut while his assigned ship waited to enter it and the shaft inside. "That's amazing that it still works after so long a time lying dormant."

Doug joined in: "When those robots are moving around in the tunnel, doing whatever they are programmed to do, they probably turn the lights on frequently. Then, if they are arranged like they were on the Moon, the lights time out and turn back off."

Mentar's deep voice filled the radios: "There will be motion sensors in the tunnels that keep the lights on as long as anyone is present and moving around, if the main feed is still intact. And here, apparently, it is."

"Gentlemen," Marvin said, "let's proceed." He looked across the shaft at the stairs system. They zigzagged from top to bottom of the shaft. He initiated a descent and Shuttle One moved slowly to the floor below, then turned toward the west to one of the tunnel openings. As far as they could see, the tunnel was bare floor, walls, and ceiling. There were lights every hundred feet or so as far as they could see. Marvin eased the ship forward into the tunnel. Guppy 1 followed, then the three shuttles.

The Armada flew along the tunnel. It was straight as an arrow into the distance until the human eye could no longer distinguish its dimensions. At a thousand feet in, there was an opening in the left hand wall.

Marvin slowed and approached the doorway cautiously then eased Shuttle One into the room. When the interior of the chamber came into view he stopped the ship and held. It was about a hundred feet on a side and fifty feet high. Inside there were robot bodies standing next to all three of the walls. Each one of the machines had a square hole recessed into its chest. The bodies were a polished gun-metal color with general human-like features and stood about twelve feet tall. The visual receptors; a screen-like material, fully circled their heads.

"I count sixty-eight of them," Doug said.

"This is their stockpile of robots," Marvin said. "It looks like they would program a brain, insert it into that slot in the chest, and put them into service."

Mentar looked over at Kronos and nodded then put on his helmet. Kronos followed suit. Mentar and Kronos checked their suits for readiness then addressed Marvin. "Colonel, I'd like to exit the ship and look at that room."

"Jake, open the doors for Mentar and Kronos,"

Jake touched down in the hallway and opened he cargo bay doors. Mentar and Kronos exited the guppy and stepped around Shuttlecraft One into the storage room. Their bulk dwarfed the robots. He stepped over to the far wall, reached down, and picked up one of the units. He turned and looked at Marvin through the windshield. "They are relatively light for their size. On Earth, about 250, maybe 300 pounds." Mentar held the robot up and examined the recessed slot in the chest in detail. "There are multiple connecting pins for the power pack and, apparently, the brain."

Kronos picked up one of the robots and examined it, then put it back down.

Mentar put the robot back in its place on the back wall of the chamber then turned to Shuttle One. "Colonel, I'd like to walk the tunnel."

"Proceed, we will follow you. Remember, you have about two hours of air."

"Understood. Kronos, let's go."

Mentar and Kronos began striding down the tunnel with the line of ships following. Colonel Ivanski, watching the two giants striding along in front to the shuttle, turned and glanced at Marvin then back to the scene ahead. "Colonel, do you trust Mentar?"

Marvin turned and looked at the Russian officer: "Yes, yes I do. Why do you ask?"

"Because I do. There's just something about him. I think he will lead his people through their plight and even out of it. I feel it."

"I agree," Marvin said. "He has asked to see President Howell. Though, I can't imagine what he has in mind."

Mentar stopped, looked around at Shuttlecraft One, then pointed ahead. There was a brighter light in the area ahead and the tunnel was getting larger. Mentar continued on. Shortly he walked into an open area. The ships, singly, flew into an immense open volume of space; the inside of one of the pyramids.

Dave spoke. "I wondered why we haven't seen lots of ruins on the surface like we found on the Moon. Here, they lived in pyramid-type structures, or, literally inside mountains."

"Probably because Mars is farther from the Sun—colder," Doug added.

Inside of the mile-high structure there were multiple floors, fifty to sixty feet apart with various-sized dwellings spread out like Earth neighborhoods. There were many support columns, stairwells, and elevator shafts. A magnificent complex that would accommodate several hundred. It appeared to be the first stop of becoming part of a planned retirement community.

Marvin keyed the radio: "Discovery, come in." There was no response. "The walls of this structure are blocking our radio signals. Shuttles Three and Four, fly around the perimeter of the building and find an opening; a doorway, and contact Discovery. One ship inside; one outside."

"On our way."

Mentar watched the two ships begin their vigil of re-establishing radio contact with the mothership, then looked upward and scanned the building. Then his eyes went to the floor and toward the center of the enormous room. "Colonel, this is the retirement center. There will be several of these structures around the planet, but this will be the one where the new arrivals are housed, initially. This is where the records center will be."

Marvin paused a moment. "There's going to be lots of bodies here, isn't there."

Mentar looked around at the Shuttle One then nodded slowly. "As far as we know, there were no units, animation units, here for our people. All of that was being done on Earth's moon.

"Mentar, do you think your young people will handle this harsh reality?"

"They have been well counseled of what they are likely to find. However, Meta, Kronos, myself, and Mayan will monitor their search closely. They must face the truth."

"Yes, they do," Marvin said. "They have no choice."

"Colonel, this is Frank, come in please."

"Ah," Marvin said, "the linkup."

"Frank, this is Marvin, we have verified the lab and a tunnel system. We traced one of them and are, right now, in one of the retirement centers. We also discovered a storage room and some of the robots that have not been activated. We are going to locate the active robots and determine what they are doing before we let these young giants begin searching through this retirement center."

"Roger, Colonel, we'll be standing by here."

"Frank, just to exercise due caution, we will be out of radio contact for a short time. The entrance to the tunnels where we are, is in the middle of the structure covered by the face, under a Quonset Hut."

"Quonset Hut?"

"Yeah. It's a structure shaped exactly like one, centered over the tunnel entrance."

"Interesting. We'll be standing by, Colonel."

"Mentar, let's backtrack to the lab and check out the opposite tunnel. I want to locate those robots we saw on the way here. It could be a long trek; you and Kronos should board the guppy."

Mentar nodded then he and Kronos entered the guppy for the flight.

With that, Marvin recalled shuttles three and four, then led the way back through the tunnel system to the lab.

The east tunnel was bare as far as they could see. Marvin flew down the tunnel as a brisk pace. A mile went by, then two; then the size of the tunnel enlarged as the west tunnel had. Marvin slowed, then stopped the ship. Jake quickly landed the guppy and Mentar and Kronos exited and looked at the entrance to a large chamber.

"Mentar," Marvin said, "what's the time on your air supply?"

Mentar looked at the inside of his left wrist. "One hour 20, Colonel."

"Okay," Marvin said, "continue."

Mentar approached the chamber with caution, standing in the door and surveying the large room. Most of its volume was bare floor. Toward the back of it there were three rows of glass crates; much smaller versions of the crates that he and Kronos and many of their own had slept in for thousands of years. These were 2 x 4 x 8 feet in size and lined across the back wall of the 1000-foot-square chamber. They were spaced 10 feet apart all the way down the far wall with a 20-foot aisle between the wall and the first row of units. There were two complete rows and a third that was about two thirds filled. He counted sixty crates in the full rows and forty-two in the unfinished one. A total of a hundred and sixty-two units. Below them was the well-known plumbing connecting them to a supply of the special gas.

Mentar glanced toward Shuttlecraft One then approached the closest unit and looked inside. He smiled then turned to the windshield of Shuttle One and gestured with a thumbs up. Marvin eased the ship over to the container and positioned it to view the interior. It was a human, normal size, that appeared to be asleep and in good shape. He noted the reddish skin, the dominant nose, and hairless face. They were clothed in the same garb as the giants had been.

Marvin looked around the chamber again. "No evidence of the robots." he said.

"Colonel, the two that we saw briefly on the surface were carrying an object about the same size as the cakes of the special gas being stored of the moon.

I think we will find them if we trace this plumbing to its source."

"Agreed," Marvin said.

Mentar began examining the base of the walls for incoming piping. Kronos went the opposite direction. When he reached the back side of the chamber he stopped and hailed the group. "Over here!"

Mentar, with shuttle one following, walked across the chamber between the containers. Kronos pointed at a larger pipe coming through the wall. Multiple pipes came from it and went across the floor to the units spaced around the chamber. Mentar checked the wall for several feet in both directions from the incoming piping. There was no opening.

"Okay," he said. "It's coming from the other side of this wall. We are about two miles from the lab entrance. We will have to go up top and find an access."

"Okay," Marvin said. "You and Kronos board the guppy and we'll go topside and check in with Discovery, then proceed with the investigation.

The Armada filed out of the tunnel, up the open shaft, and exited the half-moon-shaped end of the Quonset Hut. Marvin contacted Frank onboard Discovery with an update and notice of the next objective. Marvin led the investigative group out of the lab and up to 500 feet altitude, then, passing near Discovery, began a search east for an access to whatever was feeding the gas to the suspended animation chamber.

The sixteen students, Deck 4, lined the port holes of Discovery and watched the five ships fly by toward the east. They were thinking, *"Mentar knows what he is doing. He will tell us when we can look for our parents."*

When the Armada cleared the face, Marvin descended down toward ground-level, to fifty feet altitude. The terrain was relatively flat for over a mile. In the distance there was what looked like a giant tent, or irregular pyramid. It was pyramid-shaped but had a long apex—about a quarter-mile. As they got closer, the height became evident as well. It was at least a mile high with a base a mile square. Closing on the mountain-sized structure, Marvin resumed 500 feet altitude and began to circumnavigated it. Approaching from the west he turned to the right and flew around to the south side, searching the base for an opening. Abruptly, he stopped and held. Ahead was a lava tube that connected the wall of the structure.

Doug's eyes followed it away from the structure. "I wonder if that's the same tube we saw on our way here."

"Maybe, Colonel Ivanski responded. "It looks the same."

"If so," Marvin added, "those robots are probably in there. Okay, gentlemen, we need an open doorway to get inside. Mentar, check your air."

"Twenty-six minutes."

"That's too close since we don't know what we will find. Let's return to Discovery and change your tanks. We can have a meal and then continue on from here."

Mentar removed the pressure suit and turned it over to maintenance for service. When he ascended the stars to Deck 4 he was barraged with questions. He held up his hand and the students got quiet. "So far, we haven't seen any bodies. We did not go into the retirement quarters, yet. Apparently, they went on alert when the meteors began arriving and closed up everything in hopes of surviving the onslaught. However, it was too great and it ripped away the atmosphere of the planet, suffocating them."

There were visible reactions among the students. "Nothing could have been done," Mentar sympathized. "We all have to face the real truth.

When this horrendous tragedy happened we were very lucky because of where we were and, of course, the little ones finding us when they did." Mentar looked across the concerned faces. "As soon as we resolve the issue with the robots here I want each of you to see if you can find your parents and then look for something you can take back and keep in memory of them. They must be remembered. You must deal with this and move on. We have a future to build."

The students got quiet with their faces showing question and hope. Mentar began describing the lab, the tunnels, the entrance into the lobby of the retirement center, and the *find* of the little ones sleeping in the underground chamber as they themselves were on the Moon. Then he answered many questions and listened to voiced concerns.

Marvin, knowing that contact with the robots was imminent, restructured the excursion party to return to the investigation. He moved Doug and Dave to Shuttlecraft Two and then, with them, included Akio and Bernard, two A. I. programmers. Namiko and Daniel were added to the crew of Shuttle One. All other shuttles remained on Discovery. Marvin notified Maggie to ready Guppy 2 without the seats for possibly transporting the robot bodies back to Discovery, then went up the stairs to Deck 4 and suggested that Mentar take additional help with him to face the robots. Mentar agreed.

Mentar picked Kronos and Juno, Kronos' friend, one of the first giants to be brought to Earth, and Juno's friend, Nycron, to accompany himself.

When the four ships exited Discovery, Roger glanced at Guppy 1 carrying the two extra giants along with Mentar and Kronos. "You expecting trouble, Colonel?"

"Not really," Marvin responded. "If we were in a military setting here, real or robots, there would have been sentries posted and guards present. But, if there's an issue, I liked the way Mentar and Kronos picked up those robot bodies. If the units react to us in a threatening way, they could handle it easily."

Shuttles One and Two and Guppies 1 and 2 returned to the elongated mountain housing the piping system, and, apparently the gas supplying the units occupied by the *little ones* of Mars. They proceeded to circumnavigate the base of the structure looking for access. On the third side of the search, the north side, an opening appeared. It was the standard dimensions as all the others. It was almost completely closed by drifted sand. Mentar signaled for Guppy 1 to land and allow him and his three colleagues to exit the ship and clear the sand for entry. Marvin gave it the nod. Mentar and company donned their helmets and checked their suits. Jake promptly landed his vehicle and opened the cargo bay doors.

In less than half an hour the giants had the entrance cleared and entered the structure. Jake left the cargo bay doors open in case the giants would need to board quickly. The group stared in awe at the contents inside. There were crates of all sizes stacked up to half a mile high. Mentar examined the crates, reading the stenciling on the side of them, in Moon language. Of the multiple crates he could see from the ground level, these were containers filled with tools and equipment used to build a basic infrastructure to start a civilization. Everything you would need for the growing of food, the manufacture of clothing, assembly of shelter, facilitating transportation, and the provision of medical care. The basic needs of any society. Mentar pointed toward the multiple stacks of containers. "Those are standard shipping crates commonly used on Solaris 4."

"Supplies," Doug said. "They were stockpiling supplies for the journey home."

"That ship at Saturn," Dave added, "must be a big as they claim to hold all this stuff."

"I'll bet we find a lot more," Roger said. "It's a long way to the stars, and when you finally get there, you would need enough supplies to jump start a civilization."

"Colonel," Mentar said, "the equipment feeding the chamber next door will be across the building and to the right."

"We'll follow you. First, Mentar, all four of you check your oxygen reading. Clearing that sand from the entrance would increase usage."

Mentar looked at his and all three of the others' gauges. "Just under two hours, Colonel."

"Okay, let's check out the support equipment and perhaps the tenders of it: the robots."

Mentar and his team walked four abreast down a two-hundred-foot wide aisle between the huge stacks of shipping crates, occasionally looking up at them and at the apex of the building far above. Mentar pointed up ahead. An aisle went off to the right. They made the turn and continued on. The stacked crates, looming above them, numbered in the thousands.

After a couple of minutes of brisk walking, Mentar and company walked out into a clear area, then stopped and looked around. Just to their right was an enormous column, fifty feet diameter, that went all the way to the ceiling; the apex of the structure. It gradually got smaller in diameter the farther skyward it went. It appeared to be very small at the ceiling. There was a set of stairs circling it that spiraled all the way up to the top. Mentar looked around. The crewmembers of Shuttle One were staring at it.

Marvin addressed the group: "Everybody standby. We'll see what's at the top of the stairs. There must be a reason why they are there." Marvin and crew ascended beside the column the mile to the topmost region of the building. At the top of the column there were four platforms mounted on it, so arranged to be facing the slanted wall of the apex. At that point there was a panel that appeared to be mounted where one could slide it aside and have a visual outside. Shuttle One descended back to the floor.

"Observation platforms," Marvin said. "Four of them."

"That's a lot of stairs to climb to get to the observation deck," Doug said. "There's got to be an elevator inside the column."

Juno and Kronos walked around the column in opposite directions. Juno called out for the opposite side of it. "Here's a door. It's about fifteen feet tall." The group moved around the column for a look at the entrance.

"It must be for the little ones." Juno said.

"No," Mentar said. "Doors for the little ones are about eight feet tall. The robots are twelve feet tall; it must be for them."

"Why would they climb up to the top of the building; sentries or look-outs?"

"Power," Doug said. "They are going up there to recharge themselves."

"There are ports up there that would open to the Sun."

"Where are the robots?" Roger said.

Mentar, looking over the top of Shuttlecraft One, pointed toward the southwest, toward the wall adjacent to the chamber of the sleeping little ones. "There," he said. "Two of them are headed this way."

All pilots quickly rotated their ships for a visual. Two of the robots, the same as those observed in the lava tube were walking toward the huge column, one behind the other. They were several hundred feet away. "Mentar," Marvin said hurriedly, "perhaps you should board the guppy."

"We'll be fine, Colonel. We can always unplug them; simply pull their power packs."

"Okay," Marvin agreed. "All ships to fifty feet altitude. Jake, Maggie, those guppies are rugged. Close your outer doors and standby. Just in case we get a dangerous surprise, be prepared to ram those robots."

"Understood, Sir," the guppy pilots responded.

Mentar, Nycron, Juno, and Kronos stepped out of a line of sight path of the robots advancing toward the column. As the robots got closer, Mentar issued instructions: "Make no provocative motion. Let's see what they are going to do."

As they walked by, apparently on their way to the column, they were in exact lockstep with each other. When they arrived at the stairs circling the column, the lead robot began the climb; the other positioned himself several steps behind the leader, remaining in military cadence of the lockstep. They spiraled the column at a brisk pace, getting ever higher. Mentar, watching the robots begin their ascent of the stairs, said, "Notice that each of them had a knob in the middle of his chest, about four inches in diameter. It's a handle for removing their brain and power supply."

"They're going after a recharge." Doug said. "Apparently, the elevator isn't working."

"Wonder how long it takes them to recharge?" Daniel said. "It's mid-afternoon. They have about four more hours of sun before nightfall and it will take them about twenty minutes or so to make the climb."

"Those ports up there were on the west side of the building," Namiko added. "They would have to recharge in the afternoon."

"Mentar," Marvin said into the radio, "don't forget to keep a check on you air." Marvin saw Juno, Kronos, and Nycron quickly look at the left wrists. Mentar glanced at his. "We have almost an hour left. Colonel, let's check the area the robots came from and see if there's more of them."

"Acknowledge, we'll follow." All ships descended to ten feet and proceeded to follow the four giants walking across the floor toward some type of equipment complex in the distance. As they got closer, the equipment, covering about a city block area, became distinguishable shapes. Suddenly, Mentar stopped. "Colonel, I see movement. I count four more of the robots. They are doing something with the equipment.

"Standby," Marvin said. "Shuttle Two, follow me; ascend to a hundred feet and let's fly over the area and see what's happening."

Marvin eased Shuttle One toward the activity ahead, ascended to a hundred feet and continued forward. Lucas, in Shuttle Two, flew in formation with Shuttle One. At a hundred feet from the equipment Marvin and Lucas held. Marvin keyed the radio: "These guys are loading a block, just like the one we saw in the lava tube, into a rectangular bin or vat. It has a huge lid that's standing open. There are two of the vats mounted side by side. The other one is closed. Hold a minute, I want to check something."

Marvin flew around the spread of machinery toward the east wall of the building. "Just as I thought. There are pipes coming out of the machinery and going through the east wall. This machinery, operated by these robots, is supplying life support to the humans next door in that chamber."

Marvin returned to the observation vantage point and held. "Mentar, Guppies, come on over to our position."

The robots finished installing the block and closed the lid of the vat. Marvin noted that when the lid was completely closed the robot shifted a lever from leaning toward the second vat to leaning toward the vat just loaded. "That block is the sleeping gas, Moon gas. They stored it well away from the metropolis or living quarters and lab, apparently for safety. These robots bring in more gas as it's needed.

"This is a test that's been set up," Doug said. "They may not have been planning to take the little ones, ah, humans with them when they head for Alpha Centauri. They were using them to see if the system worked well enough to get them to the stars safely.

"I would say it's proven," Dave added. "It kept the giants alive and well for thousands of years and

Roger alive and well for twenty-six years, and now these people which appear to be okay."

"Mentar," Marvin said. "We are going to have to wake up these people and get them safely in Discovery, then shut down these robots."

"Understood, Colonel," Mentar said.

"Let's not interrupt their operation until we have all of the sleeping subjects awakened and safe," Marvin added. "Right now, let's return to Discovery and plan the operation."

Guppy 1 landed and opened its cargo bay. Mentar and company boarded. The Armada preceded to fly back toward the entrance, pausing to look up the huge column staircase. The robots were two-thirds of the way to the top. The four ships resumed and returned to Discovery.

An exaggerated silhouette of a hominid face stretched miles toward the east as the distant sun approached the western horizon. Above the elongated nose shadow was a miles-long shadow, of Discovery. Rescue had arrived. Tomorrow, once again, Discovery would extend a helping hand across the millenniums.

Chapter 8

THE AZTEC

Mexico, home of one and a half million *cousins* of the one hundred sixty-two Nahautl-speaking souls discovered on Mars, was scrambling to make policy, arrangements, and accommodations to receive the ancient peoples that were their own. It would seem that such a small number of new citizens would literally disappear in such a vast base of like-peoples. However, 50,000 years is a long time and the peoples involved were, no doubt, very different, and would be an attraction on the planet for some time. There would be many study groups, scientists, writers, historians, anthropologist, and the curious for many years to come. The basic core of a culture would be refreshed. A team of psychologists, Nahautl speaking, was being trained in the basic core of the language to work with the ancient survivors. It was expected that such a transition from a very remote past to current day would be a formidable task. The task of bringing back to Earth those that had been chosen to sleep with the gods.

Ship's stores laid out the equipment for detaching and bringing the glass crates aboard. Considering the number of units to be moved, having the giants to load them in the chamber, and some of the giants on board Discovery to unload them into the lab for awakening, the team would be able to get them all aboard in one day. Each Guppy could move ten of the units at a time.

It was decided to bring two units aboard initially and awaken them. It would be a check of the system and a check of the reaction that the human-sized people would experience when taken out of a deep sleep of thousands of years. Second; the linguists could acquaint them with their situation and then have them assist in helping the others understand what was happening to them.

Mentar assigned Juno and Nycron to work with the lab in the receiving process of the crates into the lab.

Jake readied Guppy 1 with the equipment and, accompanied by Guppy 2 with Mentar and Kronos aboard, flew to the chamber to transfer two of the sleeping Aztecs to Discovery. Shuttles One and Two flew fore and aft of the two transports. Jake entered the chamber and positioned Guppy 1 with the cargo bay doors near the crates in the outmost partial row.

Maggie entered the chamber, flew to the left of the door, touched down and opened the cargo bay doors for Mentar and Kronos. They exited the ship and joined Jim and Dennis waiting at the crates. Jim turned off the T-handle valve, then cut the line attached to the crate as he had done many times on the Moon. Dennis attached the portable pressure equipment, now preset with the necessary pounds per square inch, then the two applied the securing straps on the lids. Then Mentar and Kronos carefully moved the two crates into the cargo bay of Guppy 1 for transport to the hangar bay of Discovery. Jake immediately lifted off the chamber floor and headed for Discovery, accompanied by Shuttle One.

Karen, Jean, Professor Liggins, and the two giants, Juno and Nycron, waited in anticipation for the ancient humans to be brought into the lab. They watched Guppy One, with the precious cargo aboard, enter the open hangar bay and touch down. The doors closed and the hiss of pressurization occurred. In less than a minute, the bay had equalized and the air lock doors between the bay and the lab opened. The assigned team, the giants, Juno and Nycron, carefully picked the up the glass crates and moved them into the lab. They sat them down and stepped to the back of the lab. The maintenance team entered and removed the pressure equipment, the securing straps, then the lids, and exited the lab.

Karen, with her mobile translator at the ready, waited for the two sleeping forms to awaken from their long sleep. A minute went by, then two, as the group watched in anticipation. When the clock approached three minutes, one of the subjects stirred, then tried to turn on his side and draw up his legs.

Karen looked at Jean. "They come out from under the gas into regular sleep."

The awakened figure's knees hit the side of the glass crate and jarred him to wakefulness. He raised his head up and looked around and spotted the other crate with its lid also gone. He raised up on his elbow and starred at it, then looked around the room. He spotted Juno and Nycron standing at the back of the lab near the air lock door. "Quetzalcoatl!" The Aztec Indian jumped out of the crate, went to his knees, then bowed with his face to the floor. His fellow sleeper awakened, looked up, saw them as well, and joined him in the posture of god-like worship.

"Oh My God," Jean exclaimed, "they think the giants are gods."

Karen turned to Juno, motioned for him to lean down close to her, then spoke: "Tell them, in English, that they must not worship you, that you are not a god. The translator will change your words to Nahautl."

Juno and Nycron looked at each other, then Juno repeated, in his deep resonant voice, the words Karen had spoken quietly to him. The two Aztecs raised their heads up and looked at the giants again, then around the room and became aware of the people, their size, in the room. Their faces showed complete and utter confusion. Karen quickly began speaking to them through the translator. "We are here to take you back home. You are okay. Everything's going to be fine. You will be reunited with your people."

The two Aztecs slowly got to their feet. The first that had awakened spoke: "Where are our people?"

Karen measured her words: "We are going to bring some of them here, today. The others are in a faraway place. When we get your group all here, we will take all of you back to your people in the faraway place." Karen paused a moment, then: "I need your help."

The two Aztecs straightened up and looked at each other then back at Karen, Jean, and the others. Karen continued: "We are going to bring your group here ten at a time." The men's faces displayed more confusion. Karen continued: "I must ask you to trust me. As your people arrive and are awakened as you were, they are going to be confused and afraid. I want you to tell them that we are taking all of you home."

"I see an OK," Professor LIggins offered, studying the faces of the two ancient Aztec people. "They seem to be understanding you. However, they are overwhelmed, obviously, so we should bring the first group and see how it goes with them."

Professor Liggins keyed the radio. "We are ready for the first group. Colonel Andrews, they won't be awake very long until they are going to need food. Shall we distribute them on the three lounges and the cafeteria?"

"Good idea. You should probably take the time to get the first group settled in as well as possible, then distribute them in the four locations. If they went into shock or mental overload, it could get serious. They suddenly have a new reality."

"My thoughts as well," Karen responded. "Have the guppies bring us the first ten."

"Guppy One," Marvin ordered, "bring in the first group of the Aztec people."

Mentar watched the team shut off the gas flow to the human-sized crates, then quickly sever the connecting pipe, reestablish pressure with their portable units, then Kronos pick up the glass crate and carefully place it in the Guppy's cargo bay.

His people, his society's leaders, had arranged this test using these little ones from Earth. When their equipment was designed and ready, they simply went to Earth, landed, and instructed the little ones to enter their ship and brought them here and used them for verification of their suspended animation equipment. The little ones would comply because they assumed that his people, the scientists, were gods because of the enormous size, comparatively.

The little ones of Discovery had a sense of right-doing regarding such matters, a position of which Mentar was in agreement. There was something special about it. Since fate had arranged a restart of their society, change was definitely in their future. He would see to it.

The two awakened Aztecs reacted with a start when the hissing of pressure equalization began. When it stopped and the large air lock door slowly opened, Juno and Nycron quickly moved the ten glass containers into the lab. The two Aztecs backed up against the wall and watched. When the pressure units were removed and the lids were taken off the crates, the two Aztecs slowly walked over to the crates and looked one to the other. When their people begin to stir, they would shake them awake and begin a verbal exchange with them. The presence of Juno and Nycron was explained ten times as the subjects became wide awake and aware of their surroundings.

Ten more were brought aboard and awakened to join the twelve now waiting in the lab. When they were awake and cognizant the team spent an hour counseling the group, asking them to help expedite bringing the remainder of their people aboard. Then the team placed four of them in each lounge and four in the cafeteria, leaving six in the lab for receiving each group. Then the Guppies expedited the transfer of the remainder of the little ones that had slept in an underground chamber for millenniums, being tended by dedicated robots, whose diligence was simply running a program over and over again.

Discovery buttoned up the hatches for the night. The Aztecs were fed and moved to the main deck. The orientation was ongoing with all of the guests of Discovery, the fourteen from around the globe, approaching and visiting with the new 162 now aboard. They seemed to be adjusting very well considering the time they were out of circulation. Being greeted in their own language helped to smooth things. Knowing who they were from the records discovered on the Moon was a big plus.

Mentar enjoyed being part of a gallant rescue simply because it was the right thing to do. His fellow giants picked up on his feelings and were beginning to develop a strong allegiance to Mentar as their leader. Mentar, on his nightly radio communication with Giant City, Earth, described the day in detail to the remainder of their population, beginning to instill into them a will to follow. He was slowly becoming more that just a Counselor.

DAN HOLT

Chapter 9

THE ROBOTS

Marvin, sitting in the Captain's chair, watched the Sun peep over the reddish horizon. Day three was beginning. Following breakfast, the first order of the day would be to have Mentar and associates shut down the six operating robots in preparation for bringing their bodies on board, along with the sixty-eight bodies in the storage chamber, when Discovery was ready to return to Earth. The giants would bring the robots' power packs and brain assemblies on board immediately for study by Discovery's onboard experts.

Karen, Jean, Professor Liggins and his assistants set up a classroom therapy session for the Aztecs. To jump from cave dwellers experimenting with huts to space flight is a giant leap for the human mind to absorb. The team wanted to attempt to fill in the giant gap that they skipped over while sleeping. Many therapy sessions would be needed to help the ancient people accept what had happened to them.

Mentar, Kronos, Juno, and Nycron boarded Guppy 1, now refitted with seats. Guppy 2, now cleared for cargo, would accompany the Armada. Shuttles One and Two flew escort as the four ships made their way to the above-ground structure housing thousands of tons of supplies and the special support equipment for star travel. Shuttle One led the group through the entrance and down the aisle to the intersection, then to the right. They preceded until they reached the huge column. Shuttle One stopped the ships. "Standby," Marvin said then ascended to the apex again and checked the platforms. All were empty; all the viewing ports were closed. He descended back to the floor and headed for the machinery in southeast quadrant of the building.

Mentar spoke: "Colonel, let us get out of the ship and on our feet before we approach them. They may have a very serious grip with those specially designed hands. It's possible that they could puncture our pressure suits."

"Understood," Marvin responded then gave the order. The four giants exited the Guppy and got to their feet. Marvin keyed the radio: "Jake, stand ready to receive them back into the cargo bay and quickly pressurize if we have such an occurrence. Maggie, stand ready as well and back him up." Both pilots acknowledged.

Mentar and company approached the machinery. They spotted four of the six robots standing side by side on a raised platform adjacent to the two vats. The platform was ten feet tall putting the robots about even with the giant's waist. Mentar approached the platform and simply reached up and grasped the knob of the nearest robot and pulled the programmed unit out of the robot's chest. The robot didn't move. Mentar picked him up and put him down of the floor of the structure. He then proceeded to disable the other three. He put the first one back on the platform and then turned toward Shuttle One and smiled.

"Well," Marvin said, "that was easy enough. Where are the other two?"

Mentar looked around in all directions. "I don't see them."

"They're not at the charging stations," Doug said, "that leaves one place they are likely to be."

"In the lava tube," Dave added, "or at the other end of it, in that mound."

"We have to locate them and disable them before we move on to other things," Marvin said. "Okay, J.D., take us to the mound and let's see if they are there. Mentar, you fellas board the guppy and let him pressurize to save your air until we get there."

J.D., Shuttle One, led the group out of the storage and maintenance structure, and across the face-like building, past Discovery, then on to pick up the lava tube and begin following it. As they followed the worm-like tube they passed several breaks in the integrity of the passageway. All eyes in the ships carefully noted the tracks in each gap and searched for the robots themselves. It was assumed that they were bringing more of the caked gas cubes to maintain the Aztecs in their ongoing test of the equipment. So far there was no visual on the two missing robots. Miles later, they came to the mound at the end of the passageway. J.D. stopped the ship and held. "This is it, Colonel."

"Okay, let's see if we can find an entrance."

J.D. turned to the right and began a flight path about fifty feet from the wall of the mountain. Halfway around the mound, an entrance came into view. It was the standard dimensions as observed on all the others. J.D. proceeded to the center of the open entranceway and held. "Colonel, it's dark in there."

Marvin surveyed the perimeter of the doorway. "Let's land and let Mentar and his group exit the guppies and get on their feet and enter the doorway. Then, turn on all the ship's lights. Mentar, Juno, Kronos, and Nycron stepped into the mountain-sized mound. Shuttle One turned on its outside lights, illuminating the area near the entrance. Marvin swiveled the searchlight. There were stacks of the cakes of sleeping gas in a wax-like form towering up toward the ceiling.

"My God," Dave said, "there must be hundreds of thousands of those wax cakes of gas stored here."

The giants entered the open entranceway of the mound and began their way down the aisle leading toward the center of the building. At two hundred feet into the structure they saw two of the giant's mummified remains lying at the edge of the aisle against the stacks of wax-cake blocks. They hurried to them and examined the carcasses. It was a male and a female.

"Are they two of the scientists, Mentar?" Marvin asked.

"I think they were probably two of the retirees out for a walk," Mentar said, "and when they were informed of the disaster they took refuge in here. The residual gas present in the mound must have put them to sleep. Then when Mar's atmosphere was destroyed they died while sleeping."

Juno and Nycron seemed to be visibly shaken by the appearance of the corpses. Mentar noticed their discomfort. "You are going to see lots of this when you and the rest of the group begin searching the retirement center." They nodded.

Mentar and his three students continued walking down the aisle from the entranceway toward the center of the building. The four ships followed. The lights from the ships cast long shadows of the giants out ahead of them. A mile into the structure the aisle continued on. On each side, the wax-cakes were stacked far above them. The sheer volume of the substance indicated a plan of many years of travel under its influence. Nearing mile two, Mentar stopped abruptly, then pointed toward the left. "Colonel, there's activity near the wall of the structure. The lights are on over there. In that area, the stack of wax-cakes is much lower. I think we are going to find the other two robots working in that area."

"How do they get the wax-cakes off the top of the stack and to the floor?" Doug said.

Mentar turned toward the area of activity and approached it. The three students followed; then the ships. In a few minutes Mentar stopped and turned toward Shuttle One. "I see the two robots. They are working with a piece of equipment. It has cables on it that go up all the way to the top of the structure.

Doug glanced at Marvin; "That's it. That's got to be a crane for handling these blocks."

As the group approached the robots they saw them operating a windlass winch, lowering a block of the material to the surface. Mentar watched and waited until the block was safely on the floor, then he reached down and unplugged the two units from the robots. They became motionless in their tracks.

"Okay," Marvin said, "Maggie, let Kronos put the two robot bodies into your Guppy."

"Yes, Sir," Maggie responded and opened the cargo bay of the guppy. Kronos slid the two robot bodies into it.

Mentar and the team surveyed the structure past the crane and the acres beyond. "They have used thousands of these blocks," Doug said. "Look at the stack across the aisle and compare it to the height of the other stacks. I wonder how long one block lasts when supplying 162 sleepers?"

"Good question," Marvin answered. "I would think it would be a long time; 50,000 years is a long time be under its influence. I'll say this: these robots are reliable. They have tended to the 162 humans for thousands of years without a failure. They will be the subject of a lot of study when we get them back home."

The four ships circumnavigated the interior of the storage structure. They noted the lava tube entrance being used for a transit conduit to the lab, then another entrance was located on the opposite side of the mound from their original point of entry. The Armada began its journey back to the mother ship to conclude another day on the red planet. The onboard programmers were anxious to get their hands on the units that powered and directed the robots.

Marvin sat in his quarters deep in thought. These people were diligently preparing for a multiple year journey to the stars. He had heard Daniel and some of his colleagues talk about reaching Alpha Centauri. They had estimated that Magnetic Inertial Propulsion would reach it in about twenty-two years. It was a complicated series of acceleration and deceleration sequences that put the ship in that vicinity in just over two decades. The transit time for the giants, when they had gotten their ship restored to service, was unknown. The giants were perfecting suspended animation equipment to keep themselves from aging during the journey. That would indicate that the transit time was considerable. Therefore, they had to have someone to fly the ship; someone who could tend to it if something went wrong. At least someone that would wake up some designated crewmembers to address the problem.

They would need robot pilots, automaton pilots, to quote one of the A. I. programmers. At least they would have to be smarter than the robots they had seen so far. Marvin wondered, *"Where are they? They were not in the lab that had been explored. Is there another lab?"* Tomorrow, he would move Discovery near the entranceway of the structure, the living area they had flown into and let Mentar supervise the student's search for their parents. Frank would man the COM on Discovery. Marvin would take shuttles one and two and explore the Cydonia area around the lab. He would take the A. I. programmers, Doug, Dave, Roger, Ivan, and perhaps De Liang, the electronics guy, and search the area and try to locate another facility that was working with robots or automatons. They were here somewhere. He was sure of it.

Marvin pillowed his head. His thoughts wandered back to the day he was introduced to Magnetic Inertial Propulsion; the day his life changed, for the better. He drifted off to sleep.

DAN HOLT

Chapter 10

THE RETIREMENT CENTER

Day 4 – the day of the students

Today the students would comb the facility near the lab for their parents. So far they had no way of knowing where their parents were. However, they knew they would be in the structure near or connected to the lab, as it was on the moon. The building was designed to accommodate hundreds at a time. They would have to search floor to floor and look for them, or if the remains were completely unrecognizable, look for memorabilia that they would recognize. The task was formidable but the motivation was high.

Following breakfast and a meeting with the students by Mentar, to issue directives on behavior and responsibility, Marvin informed the ship's company and then flew Discovery to the open entrance that Shuttles One and Two had located. He landed Discovery near the entrance so that the students, in pressure suits, could begin their vigil of searching the huge retirement complex. The students donned their pressure suits and entered the air lock to be processed outside. Kronos, Juno, Mayan, and Nycron accompanied the group as Monitors. They entered the huge facility. Guppies One and Two, fitted with seats, launched and entered the building, then landed on the floor and stood by in case they were needed. The students surveyed the building then headed for the stairs and floor 2, the beginning of the lodgings.

Marvin and his selected crews boarded Shuttles One and Two and launched. They rose to 500 feet and began a flight circling the lab, looking for any structure that might house an operation similar to the lab. Perhaps there would be the place where the giants were working on sophisticated Automatons to fly their starship back to their ancient home. As the two ships flew an ever-widening pattern around the face, Marvin noticed the absence of ruins on the surface. Mars, a cold planet, supported a civilization that had learned the best way to deal with cold. They simply lived inside the mountains to have their insulation against the permanent cold atmosphere. They tunneled from mountain to mountain for protected travel from one to the other. Their survey continued on.

Inside the retirement center

The students began walking the aisles. They spread out, two or three taking an aisle, then the rest proceeding to the next aisle and three more turning down it, walking along and looking in the doors on each side of the hallway. Each accommodation was 200 feet square with two rooms in the back, each a hundred feet square. In almost every one there was mummified remains in various positions.

Almost an hour into the search a cry of success came over the radio. A student had found his own. When he shouted his success a couple of fellow students nearby came running to his door and looked in. He pointed at a stringed instrument leaning up in the corner of the room. "My gallawane," he said excitedly.

Karen quickly checked the language computers to translate Moon to English. "A guitar," she said into the radio.

His fellow students surveyed the room. The student's parents were sitting at the kitchen table, across from each other. They were holding hands across the table; their heads had settled to the table, face down, between their arms. There was a silent moment.

"I want to leave them like that," the student said.

The students backed out of the room. The student carefully stepped around the table, and his parents, and picked up his *gallawane*, hugged it, then went back out into the hallway, paused and looked at his parents again, then headed for Discovery with his treasure.

Aboard Shuttlecraft One

Marvin could no longer see Discovery or the mountain where she was parked. The terrain had been mostly flat with a ravine or two. Now they were approaching more mountains; apparently favored dwelling places on planet Mars. The two crews studied the terrain as it passed by the ship. Marvin saw a darkened spot at the base of a mountain on the right of the ship. He signaled for a stop. He pointed out the oddity and the crew turned the ship and headed toward it for an investigation. As they approached, it became evident that it was a hollow mountain with the standard entrance door.

"Why this far away?" Marvin said and steered Shuttle One through the entrance, then into the darkened interior and turned on the ship's lights. Immediately they saw bodies strewn randomly across the spacious building. The structure had multiple floors just as the retirement center attached to the lab.

"This is a regular resident community on Mars," Doug said. "No doubt, this is going to be typical all over the planet. All these people, all giants, were taken out by the explosion of Solaris 4. The scope of that disaster is unfathomable."

"Yeah," Dave said. "And we were oblivious of it, waiting for the growth of our technology to bring us this far."

Marvin reversed course and exited the mountain-sized structure. "Let's continue our search. I want to know if the scientists had started development of Automatons for their impending journey home."

"Colonel," Roger said, "a suggestion: let's go back to the lab and check it out more thoroughly. It's likely, if they had begun working with Automatons, it would be in the programming lab. Perhaps they were working on the software itself and had not started designing the bodies of the Automatons."

"True," Marvin agreed. "Let's return and give that lab another detailed search." Marvin paused a moment, looked at the ship's chronometer, then spoke: "By way of Discovery's galley for some lunch."

Inside the retirement center

One of the five female students sounded off into the radio. "I found her, I found Mom!!" Again, the students gathered at the door of the apartment. She pointed at the right hand of the remains sitting in a chair. "Mom had an accident two years ago, uh, two years before things went wrong, and had to have her middle finger lanced. It drew up in a flexed position and stayed that way."

All of the student's eyes went to the right hand of the remains, to the permanently flexed middle finger; the identity of a loved one. Two of the other female students hugged her. She began to search through the degraded contents of the apartment and found some pieces of her mother's jewelry, with her name engraved on it, to take back home.

By noon the students had covered much of the lower section of the building. Mentar called them back to Discovery for lunch and a two-hour break. The pressure suits had to be serviced. Several others had located their parents and had claimed something of them, and their childhood home, to keep. Some of the items were simple everyday items that, now, under these circumstances had become precious. They, those who had not located their own, would be able to return and continue the vigil.

Onboard Discovery

Mentar keyed the radio and raised Giant City, Earth. Its residents were waking for the day. They began gathering around the radio in anticipation. Mentar briefly described the ongoing activity on the fourth day on Mars, then allowed the students that had located their parents and some memorabilia to speak their friends back on Earth. The chatter went on for some time despite the cumbersome delay. The beginnings of some deep healing.

Marvin and the two crews were filled in on the students' vigil. Some special moments had happened, moments that would matter. When the crews heard about the giant finding his guitar, his gallawane he'd called it, Roger Stahls spoke up: "I played guitar back in the 50's."

"This one is twenty feet long," Doug said. "I don't think you could handle it."

Roger smiled. "They said his name was Javienne. I wonder how well he plays."

Chapter 11

THE AUTOMATON

Following lunch and a reorganization, the seven students that had not as yet found their retired parents suited up to resume the difficult task of combing through the mummified remains and degraded ruins in the retirement center. They entered the airlock and were processed outside.

Marvin petitioned Mentar: "I want to further search the lab for evidence of the Automatons that the leaders of your government were in the process of developing. I want to know, for sure, the extent of their progress with them. Can the students that are searching the retirement facility be handed over to Kronos so that we can have you, Juno, and Nycron to accompany us on another search of the lab?"

"Yes, Colonel. I will have Javienne assist Kronos. Javienne has had his day; he was very lucky. They will be fine."

Shuttles One and Two, along with the Guppy 1 transporting the three giants and Guppy 2 with its empty cargo bay, launched and proceeded to the lab entrance and then inside. They, in formation, circumnavigated the interior of the face, studying the walls, the equipment stations, and tooling areas.

"So far just the one tunnel," Ivan said. "This may be as far as they had gotten with preparing pilots to steer their ship across the great void between here and Alpha Centauri."

"Maybe so," Marvin said dubiously. "They would surely be working on the programming. We will have many science missions returning here. They can research that aspect.

"Wait a minute!" Doug said, pointing upward toward the ceiling. "Look at that. It's an oval structure right where the eyes would be on the face if you were flying over it. It looks to be about a thousand feet end-to-end."

"One of the Shuttles reported that the eyes were actually landing pads." Dave noted.

Marvin lead the ascent toward the unusual structure. Upon approach an entrance came into view. Shuttle One cautiously entered the giant room. The Armada followed.

"This looks like the bridge of a ship!" Doug said.

"Training!" Colonel Ivansky said, "it's a mockup for training."

"That would mean that there's someone to train," Bernard said. "Notice that everything is giant-size. This is not for the robots that we've already encountered."

Marvin surveyed the room. "Were they training actual people, giants, or do they have automatons the size of the giants?"

"Or," Doug rejoined, "both. Look, there. There are the regular sized books and a reading machine just like the training stations we found on the Moon. Those are likely to be about the ship they're restoring."

"Colonel," Mentar said, "let us get out and look this over. They must have a training program for the computers to run simulations to train pilots whether they be real or automaton."

"Good idea," Mavin said.

Mentar, Juno, and Nycron got on their feet and began to study the layout of the training room. On one end of the oval was a mockup of a main bridge. It had six seats across a curved screen, no doubt replacing what would be a windshield, that were all the correct proportions for the forty-foot tall giants. Below the screen were all the expected gauges, readouts, controls, etc. On the other end of the facility, in the distance, was a control center for an engine room. It had flat square-shaped monitors across in front of the seats. Below them were multiple controls, knobs, meters, gauges, and tale-tell lights.

Mentar and his two associates headed for the main bridge. Approaching it, he swiveled one of the center seats, sat down in it, and swiveled it back around to face the control panel. He reached up and flipped on a toggle switch located at the base of the center monitor. The monitor lit up. It was a star field. On the screen there was a thin line pointing at a specific star with writing, in Moon, on the other end of it. There were several scattered around the display. "Navigation."

Maggie, sitting in her pilot's seat in Guppy 2, saw movement out of the corner of her eye. Her head snapped to the right. It was a forty-foot robot or automaton walking toward the group, apparently coming from the engine room control center. "Colonel!" she shouted in to the radio. "There's a robot, or one of those automatons, coming from the other end of the room. He's as big as Mentar."

All eyes went to the advancing automaton. Mentar swiveled his seat and stood. He walked toward the advancing machine; ordering Juno and Nycron to stay behind him.

Marvin studied the automaton momentarily. "Mentar, do you think you can handle him if he gets ugly?"

"I think so, Colonel. He's got a knob in the middle of his chest. Also, notice that he has a normal head and arms; shaped like us. Let's see what he's going to do."

Marvin glanced at Guppy 2. Maggie had already lined up her machine with the approaching Automaton. She flipped open the cover over the emergency button, placed her hand over it, and waited.

The automaton walked up to Mentar, stopped ten away, looked him up and down, then turned his eyes to survey all four ships. Then, in a lightning fast move, he grabbed Mentar by the left arm and left leg and picked him up over his head.

Marvin yelled. "Maggie hit the automaton in the chest at full power."

The unit was knocked backward twenty feet onto his back. Mentar fell on top of the guppy then rolled off of it onto the floor. He quickly got to his feet and looked at the automaton lying on the floor. A wisp of blueish smoke came out of the automaton's chest cavity where the power pack had been. The power pack unit was lying on the floor halfway between the disabled automaton and Maggie's ship. There were sparks coming from it. All eyes went to Mentar. "He punctured my suit," Mentar said, speaking with effort.

"Juno, Nycron," Marvin shouted, "help Mentar and board the guppy."

They quickly did so and Jake pressurized the cargo bay. Mentar caught his breath. "Good move, Maggie. That thing caught me by surprise. Colonel, can we get those books and the reading machine back to Discovery. I'd like to study them."

"Can do," Marvin said. "Jake, take Mentar back to Discovery for a checkup then return here and have Kronos and Nycron recover that library."

Jake quickly steered Guppy 1 out the entranceway and headed for Discovery. The rest of the Armada followed.

"That Automaton's programming is faulty or not finished." Akio said. "That's the thing about A.I. programming; when you give a unit a directive like, say, *'keep this ship running smoothly;'* it takes thousands of lines of code to put limits on what they are to do."

Bernard joined in: "This automaton saw you as a problem because you changed some settings on that panel. He would have probably thrown you out the door of the bridge. His programming is too simple. When you weren't here the bridge was running smoothly. When you came, there was a problem. So, he would remove you."

Back inside Discovery

The moment the Guppie's hangar bay pressure had equalized, a medical team met Mentar. They were able to give him a clean bill of health thanks to the quick response of the team in restoring his air supply and pressure before his suit had bled down. Juno and Nycron were hailed for their actions. Jake and his crew, along with Juno and Nycron, returned to the training bridge and recovered the training books and reading machine. Maintenance began going over the structural integrity of Guppy 2's cargo bay. There was no damage; the impact had been square with the machine favoring the structural design.

In the Retirement Center

As late evening approached, the energetic students, searching ever higher in the retirement center, sounded six more successful finds. Since their parents were recent transfers to the Solaris 3 retirement center, they all were still in the initial receiving center and therefore findable. The one student that was unable to locate his was determined to begin at the floor level again.

Mentar, apprised of Mychaal's determination, deciding to take a long shot, asked to talk with Colonel Andrews privately. The two had a brief private conversation. Then Mentar and Mychaal entered Guppy 1, accompanied by Shuttle One, and flew to the sleeping gas storage mound. The ships entered and flew to the location of the remains of a couple that were discovered on an earlier excursion.

Mychaal looked at the remains lying side by side, then at Mentar. Mentar saw the fear in Mychaal's eyes. Mentar spoke: "Maybe it's them; you need to know."

The student paused a moment, then nodded.

Mentar and Mychaal exited the Guppy and approached the couple. Physical identification was impossible, however, Mychaal spotted a circular object lying beside the larger mummified body, partially covered with dust. He reached down and picked it up and wiped the dust off of it, then shouted: "Daaaaad!"

Mentar jerked in reaction then focused on the object in Mychaal's hand. He held it up for Mentar to see. "It's a medallion that I gave Dad when he reached retirement age and qualified to transfer to lower gravity," Mychaal said in a rush of words. "Can we take them back to the retirement center?"

"If you try to move them, their bodies will fall apart, down into the dust. Teams will be coming back to Mars to deal with what has happened here. Perhaps they will have a way to preserve them. They were together, Mychaal, remember them that way."

Mychaal paused a moment, looked at the medallion in his hand, then nodded. He and Mentar entered the cargo bay of the guppy and were flown back to Discovery. Mychaal showed the medallion to his fellow students and relived the moment, many years ago, when he surprised his father with a special gift.

Night fell on the very eventful day-four on Mars as the Sun approached overhead on Earth. The radio link, Deck 4 to Giant City, Earth, was abuzz as the students related their finds with their friends back on Earth. Mentar's fight with a robot was big news. Visions of adventure circulated through Giant City.

As the evening wore on the radio link settled into quietness and Mentar signed off. Karen and her team, in their daily tutoring of the Aztec people, had concluded for the day. A quietness settled on the ship with small groups scattered throughout the ship reviewing the day and the Mission so far.

The many groups gradually grew quiet as they became aware of faint sounds of music filling the ship. The purity of the tone and chords were so gripping that the supervisor of the Deck 4 galley reached up and keyed the mike open on the intercom. The melodious sounds of a ballad came from the speakers and flowed through the ship. Professor Liggins glanced at the nearest speaker in the lounge. "The tones from that instrument are so pure. It would make Antonio Stradivari jealous."

There was a cycle of notes that, a moment later, began to repeat. Then, a deep, pure, resonant, voice, singing in Moon, accompanied the music. A hush fell on Discovery. The mesmerizing ballad continued. It had the haunting appeal of *HOME SWEET HOME*. The vocalization continued for three verses then faded into silence. Discovery was dead quiet for several moments; then the atmosphere of the ship was filled with applause that lasted minutes. Javienne looked up in surprise then gripped his instrument.

Chapter 12

WHAT NOW?

Day 5

The Sun peeped over the Martian horizon introducing Day 5; light travel time 12.6 minutes. Discovery had completed her objective. The objective of determining the extent of the giant's activity on Mars related to the obvious preparations being done on Earth's moon. An understanding of what the race of giants was all about was coming together as the result of the special efforts being put forth by the *Little Ones* of planet Earth.

Eons ago they came to a virgin solar system, a special treasure, having left their home planet for unknown reasons. They chose the Solar System because of its proximity and their mother ship's failing main drive. They chose to inhabit planet number 4 of the 8 present then in the unoccupied system. The first four were blue and white worlds, pristine, clean, circular orbits, and livable atmospheres. Somewhere in the flowing of time of the society a split occurred; a parting of the spiritual and the secular. Venus became the home of the spiritual.

Then, as their numbers grew on Solaris 4, they configured planet 3 as a first step to relieve the stress of gravity on the aged. Then later, planet 2's moon, for the final years of their life. Later still, the deep inward desire to return home, over time, reconfigured the motive and drive of the society.

The labs were set up in the existing infrastructure of the retirement facilities. Work began on arranging a starship, using the original vessel for restoration, and also suspended animation to preserve the race in transit, and setting aside needed supplies to begin again at their destination.

Now, today, Discovery would load its cargo bay with the tools and machinery discovered on Mars and return to Earth.

Then there would be the: *WHAT NOW?*

The 1212 student giants rescued on the Moon were approaching adulthood. They were adjusting to their environment and life was beginning to take its natural course. One pregnancy was known and soon there would be others. There were two choices: Make room for them or help them get home. To choose the first would change planet Earth forever. However, to choose the second would also change planet Earth forever, perhaps for the better. Earth would be helping, interacting, with a galactic neighbor.

Mentar had requested a meeting with the president.

DAN HOLT

Chapter 13

THE MEETING

President Walter Howell, nearing the end of his second term, had a meeting scheduled with Mentar, leader of the giants. Mentar had requested the meeting through Colonel Andrews. Walter Howell's years of involvement in the matter of the giants told him that he was going to have one more hurdle to cross before he handed the scepter over to another. He had his staff set up the meeting with the presence of Karen, Jean, and Professor Liggins to ascertain clarity of communication. Colonel Andrews and his bridge crew, who probably knew Mentar better that anyone, were asked to attend, along with Winston Stone, head of NASA, and his staff.

Mentar had asked that his associates, Counselors Meta, Brock, and Mingee be in attendance. It was so arranged. The meeting would be held on Discovery, Deck 4, a conference area best configured to accommodate all in attendance.

The meeting was set for three weeks away to allow time for the immediate matters to be resolved. The Aztecs had to have arrangements made to assimilate them into the community of like peoples now living in Mexico. The students were returned to their friends who were waiting anxiously. And the bounty discovered and retrieved on Mars was placed at various research labs around the country for examination and evaluation.

Discovery was moored on her launching pad undergoing a complete maintenance shakedown. Carl Weathers, final inspector of the rotor pods before they are released for service, headed up the maintenance review. Frank had ordered all the main bearings of the rotor pods replaced. The old ones were to be checked with micrometers for amount of wear per running hour, if any, at this relatively early stage of operation. None of the rotor pods had failed due to mechanical problems and Frank wanted it to stay that way. The rotor pod damaged by the high speed meteorite was removed and taken to the lab for a careful examination. A replacement was added to the tool room as a backup.

All excursion craft, Shuttles and Guppies, went through the same maintenance review and update.

As the day of the meeting approached Mentar was finishing up a review of the books found on the training room where the automaton was in process of being programmed. They turned out to be a rich source of material, fit for reference in the upcoming meeting. He had a personal goal of getting the help of the little ones to arrange a journey home for him and his kind. He believed the information in the pages of these books supplied the bargaining tools he needed. This was a challenge of a lifetime. The books were a detailed account of the construction and makeup of the ancient starship parked in Saturn orbit. On that ship, if salvaged, were enormous amounts of materials used by the little ones in their present stage of development. They needed the bounty; he needed a ship. It was time for a meeting.

Mentar, during his tenure on Earth, had learned the general functioning of the society of America and it economic system. Though not fully understood he felt he knew enough to present his case, the case for his and his people's goal of getting home to the stars. Having gotten to know Colonel Andrews and his devoted crew, he looked forward to the meeting and a positive outcome.

Meeting Day

Guppy 1, configured with seats, was flown to Giant City, Kansas to pick up Mentar and colleagues and transport them to Discovery in Aurora, Illinois. Shuttles One and Two sailed across the skies of Washington D.C. to provide transportation of the president and his advisors to Aurora and Discovery.

Marvin and his bridge crew, along with Karen, Jean, and the professor and NASA, waited in Discovery's freshly-cleaned galley and cafeteria area on Deck 4 as the parties arrived and made their way to the *land of the giants*.

President Howell, seated at the greatly modified conference table, looked across at Mentar, seven times his size. The giant was seated at a table built for his size and yet the table was so arranged that when you reached the other side the table was correct for the *normal* human being. For a brief moment it seemed to Walter Howell that he was at a carnival house if mirrors looking at himself in a greatly curved mirror. He shook off the thought.

When everyone was seated, the group became quiet. There was an awkward moment as Mentar collected his thoughts. He began: "Mr. President, I want to thank you for arranging this meeting and taking the time see us. We are very grateful for the helping hand that you and the peoples of Earth have extended toward us. We find ourselves in a very awkward position here, in your country, on your planet. However, without your kindness and your superior ethics, we would not be here at all. We thank you for that."

President Howell nodded. "We were glad to help, Mentar. It's the only thing we could do. It's who we are. I must say, Mentar, it sounds like you are leaving. How…"

Mentar nodded then glanced at his fellow Counselors then back to the president. "I want to buy a starship from you—from Earth."

President Howell didn't know quite how to respond to that. He looked at Karen, the linguist, then at Marvin. Marvin looked at Mentar. "Mentar, what method of payment?"

"A hundred thousand tons, combined, of Gold, Silver, Platinum, Palladium, Ruthenium, Rhodium, Iridium, Osmium, and another several thousand tons of Copper."

"All the precious metals used in electronics," the president's financial advisor, Kyle Windom, said. "Where is all of this stuff, now?"

"It's in the salvaging of our disabled ship in orbit around your sixth planet. I just finished studying the books recovered on Mars that describe the ship, and Brock, one of our Counselors, is a historian and supplied the details I just mentioned. Your Discovery can recover it for you. The ancient ship is 900 miles in diameter. No doubt, there's even more things usable and valuable in the ship as well. At your stage of technical development these metals will benefit you greatly."

"He's right, Mr. President," Kyle responded.

"Mentar," the president said, "are you wanting to purchase Discovery?"

"No, Mr. President. Discovery, though a great ship, is too small to travel the distance we must go; to Alpha Centauri. We need a ship just like it, but four times the size, about 2400 feet in diameter to be able to carry enough supplies for such a journey."

Kyle whistled. "That would cost upwards of a trillion dollars start to finish."

President Howell glanced at his advisor. "If those metals are really there on that ship at Saturn, they would cover it. In fact, such a cache and the collective building of such a ship would stimulate the economies of all the countries involved."

"They are there," Mentar said. "We can take Discovery and verify it before we begin work on *LITTLE ONE*. That's what we will name the starship, in your honor, Sir. I've worked out the logistics on her. She, using Discovery's propulsion system, will reach our star system, Alpha Centauri, in just over twenty-two earth-years. We are all young enough that we can afford the time to get home without the suspended animation equipment. You can keep it here on Earth, research it, and possibly use it in the future to explore the stars, or, come see us, and return home without taking too many years out of your lives."

"How old are you, Mentar?" Marvin asked.

"On Earth, forty-two. My life expectancy is about a hundred and twenty in Earth years."

"Okay," President Howell said. "We are going to need to research this. Let's adjourn and meet again when we have the necessary information."

Mentar nodded and smiled.

Walter Howell spontaneously stuck his hand out toward Mentar. Mentar clasp it between his thumb and forefinger and shook it. The president looked at Mentar's hand, momentarily, then at his own, and nodded.

DAN HOLT

Chapter 14

PREPARATIONS

The president ordered NASA to verify the existence of the massive ancient starship. They would need to board the huge vessel and verify it as a starship indeed and to verify the bounty claimed by Mentar. Walter Howell knew that Mentar's word was good. However, there would be multiple nations involved on such a colossal project and all the bases must be touched.

NASA readied two padded containers, 10 x 10 x 50 feet to be stored aboard Discovery for its mission to Saturn. The containers were specifically designed to protect delicate electronic components. Also, NASA added to Discovery's supplies inventory fifty compressed air hand *guns* designed to be used as personal thrusters for maneuvering in a *Zero-G* environment, expected to be encountered in exploring an orbiting starship. The guns were a simple pistol grip with trigger and an eight-inch diameter sphere, mounted under the barrel and nozzle, filled with compressed air. The surface of the ancient ship would offer a very faint gravity, however, the interior would reach *Zero-G*. Five additional thruster units, sized for the giants, were included.

The same crew would board Discovery for the extended Mission of flying to Saturn with two exceptions. The 16 giants that were flown to Mars under special circumstances were returned to Giant City, Kansas along with Meta and Mayan. Brock, the giant Counselor and historian, a mainstay with the students from the start, would be added to the manifest for his first Mission on Discovery. The giants aboard traveling to Saturn would be Mentar, Kronos, Nycron, and Brock.

Iapetus, Discovery's objective, was known to Earth's astronomers as a moon of Saturn; the yin-yang moon; the term meaning dark—bright. One side of the moon was a charcoal black color; the other snow white colored. The moon was in tidal lock with Saturn which made it seem to disappear for half of its 79-day orbit, from Earth's viewing perspective. The discoverers simply could not see the black side of the moon until they developed better more powerful telescopes.

The giants claimed it was actually a huge space ship designed for interstellar travel. The darkened side was the bow, always facing the direction of travel. The darkened coloration was the result of high speed collisions with trillions of hydrogen atoms sparsely filling interstellar space.

Iapetus had been held in suspect as artificial by some astronomical circles on Earth because of its orbit being off plane like Pluto's orbit, and its gravity value as versus its size. Its size, 900 miles in diameter, yielded only 1/40th the gravity value of Earth. Further, the most suspicious discovery, it had a twenty-mile high ridge on its equator that circled the entire moon. The giants claimed that the ridge housed electronic equipment that generated a magnetic field of some sort that resulted in propulsion toward the blackened side of the ship.

While Discovery was undergoing maintenance, Marvin went to the local book store and purchased a copy of Gulliver's Travels by Jonathan Swift. He took it to Karen with a request for her and her team to translate it to Moon and size it for the giant's reading machines. The linguist team did so and presented the *one of a kind* gift to Marvin in two weeks. Marvin placed it in his briefcase to await an opportunity. He asked Karen about the Aztecs and their assimilation into the modern society waiting for them in central Mexico. Karen, having just returned from the region, responded enthusiastically: "Amazingly adjustable, those people. The fact that they were flown to another planet and slept with the gods, they attribute to the realm of the gods and just dismiss it. Here, they are fascinated. Everything is magic. They want to know how everything works. Some of their exploits are quite comical. All things considered, they will be fine. The human being is a very adaptable creature."

"I'm glad," Marvin said. "Everybody deserves a chance at a decent life."

"You know, Marvin, with all we have experienced in the past four plus years, I wonder if things will ever get back to normal."

"I think we are now living the new normal."

Chapter 15

THE DEDICATION

Discovery rose from the launch pad to return in two and a half months. Transit time to Saturn would be just over 34 days, then a 5-day investigation, followed by the same return time. Telemetry was a series of acceleration and deceleration segments to manage Discovery's relative speed. Upon arrival in Saturn's orbit a new program would be installed into guidance to rendezvous with Iapetus. Iapetus' orbit was two million miles from Saturn and seventeen degrees off plane. Discovery would have to match Iapetus' orbital speed of just under two miles per second, or 7000 miles per hour, then land on the Saturn side of the tidally-locked moon.

Discovery, leaving the satellite belts behind, adjusted it trajectory and marched onward to a predetermined spot in the Saturn family of moons where an intruder would be waiting.

"Colonel," Doug said, "the ancient ship is spherical. That indicates that it did not use acceleration to supply artificial gravity, unless...there's a main deck that's constructed perpendicular to the bow, the direction of travel, and the engines were capable of generating *one-g* acceleration."

Marvin glanced at Doug. "Good question. Let's go talk to Mentar." The three climbed the stairs to Deck 4. Mentar was studying one of the books he had recovered on Mars in the mockup bridge. Marvin, seeing the book, paused a moment, then hurried back down the stairs, got his briefcase and returned. The others looked at each other. Marvin laid his briefcase down, opened it, and picked up the newly minted, Moon rendition, of Gulliver's Travels.

"Mentar," he said, "I have something for you."

Mentar stared at the book, exactly of the dimensions of the book he was just studying. Then his eyes went to Marvin's face.

"I want you to have this book," Marvin said. "I had it translated into Moon and sized for your reading device. It was written about 300 years ago. It's a story about little ones smaller than me, and giants larger than you."

"Gulliver's Travels!" Doug said.

Mentar accepted the book and looked it over. "I'm looking forward to reading it."

"Now," Marvin said, "what we came to talk to you about. The ancient spaceship; was it so configured for perpetual weightless travel, or was there some type of artificial gravity?"

Mentar glanced at his library of the details of the ancient ship then back to his visitors. "The ship is equipped with a central rotating cylinder 400 miles in diameter and 400 miles across. It's centered in the ship and provided artificial gravity. Everything having to do with the personnel is inside the cylinder. Food is grown in there. Oxygen generating plants are spread throughout the cylinder. The outside hull of the ship is 20 miles thick and the drive is imbedded in that part of the ship. The hull was reinforced to stand impacts in space travel. It could not avoid them like Discovery."

"What about access?"

"It has the standard 300-by-70 feet access tunnels."

"Thank you, Mentar." Marvin and company went down the stairs.

Mentar turned and keyed his reading machine and inserted a novel.

Discovery sailed on through the cosmic night. When she passed Mars' orbit, the planet was now traveling its path far away and seemed just another star to observe. Then came the asteroid belt during which the mother ship made a couple of mild course corrections obeying the AVS system for ample clearance. The remains of Solaris 4 were now a collection of bodies, with an average of a million miles on a side, still traveling the path of a once great planet.

Next came Jupiter with its family of moons. It seemed to rotate in sequence with Discovery's passing as though saluting mankind for its accomplishment.

Discovery adjusted it trajectory toward the Saturn system and sailed onward. The relatively frequent rotations and reverse of power sequences of the ship were a clear reminder that, although Discovery had all the comforts of home, they were in fact hurling through the harsh environment of space. The managing of Discovery's velocity was to avoid overpowering the AVS system so that the ship could *see* and maneuver around space debris.

Discovery left Jupiter behind and steamed on to its rendezvous with Saturn and its eighth moon, Iapetus. Ships Records sent a message to Colonel Andrews.

Ship's Records requests the presence of Marvin Andrews, Douglas Hastings, Frank Gordon, David Henson, Daniel Stubblefield, and Roger Stahls in the aft lounge.

Marvin notified his colleagues and the group headed for the lounge. When they walked through the arched entranceway there were a large number of the ship's compliment present, standing in silence, waiting. The bridge crew noticed Robert Sheridan, head of Ship's Records, standing next to the forward wall holding a cord attached to a sheet-type covering, 10 x 20 feet, draped over something mounted on the forward wall.

Robert paused a moment, then spoke: "Gentlemen, we present to you, with the deepest honor and respect, and perhaps a little awe..."

He pulled on the cord, releasing the covering, and an eight-by-ten-foot artist rendition of a special scene appeared. The crowd cheered and applause began that lasted for several minutes. The bridge crew stared at the exquisite painting for several moments. It was a scene set by their original voyage and return from the Moon in Research One, the original spaceship that began the saga. The ship was sitting on the tarmac of the original Earth Base One. The ramp was open and there were seven souls standing at the base of the ramp. Their likenesses were exquisite. Roger Stahls was standing in the center just forward of the ship's crew. To his left and behind him was Marvin Andrews, Daniel Stubblefield, and Isaac Henson. To his right was Frank Gordon, Douglas Hastings, and David Henson.

The caption read: **RESEARCH ONE**

The mural would forever grace the wall of Discovery's main lounge.

The days turned into a week, then two, as Discovery sailed onward. The crew planning and re-planning their approach to investigating the ancient ship and its contents. Mentar related all that he was able to deduce from the writings stored on Mars and subsequently confiscated for study. The giant's ship was a vessel of a remarkable design. It was apparently constructed for long duration expeditions, possibly even across the galaxy but landed in the Solar System due to a major failure of the main drive. A drive that, over the coming years, would be studied in depth.

Week four began and Saturn began to dominate the view for the spacefarers. Curiosity began to grow in the ranks. Mankind always had to know. Explorers all.

As Discovery approached the system, telemetry engaged the final program, a program derived from observation and verification from Earth's computers. Discovery adjusted it heading and approached Iapetus at a thirty-degree angle and a speed that resulted in parallel flight with the moon when it passed into its away-from-the-Sun side of its orbit. Discovery steered itself to the inward surface and approached the moon. The program announced its release of the helm to the pilot. Marvin and Frank flew her closer and closer until they were able to pick a landing spot relatively smooth and level.

Discovery touched down on the surface of the ancient ship, once thought to be a moon. As a precaution, Doug set the customary *flying at ground level* instruction to the control computer.

Ship's Records reported to Earth Base Discovery's arrival and landing. Signal travel time was now one hour and eleven minutes. Soon after Discovery had launched and widened the gap between itself and Earth, a commentary began to keep Earth informed of the Mission's progress in a respond-later format. Now, upon arrival, a two-way conversation was a two-and-half-hour ordeal.

Although the transit from Earth was filled with multiple *Zero-G* sessions of four-minutes duration, a readiness training program of sorts, the faint gravity of Iapetus soon became noticeable. Determination, focus, and discipline became the order of the day to complete this mission.

Marvin called an organizational meeting on Deck 4. Mentar was given the floor to inform the explorers of the information he'd been able learn so far from the library.

According to the drawings and write-up of the specifications on the ancient ship, there were access ports scattered around the circumference of the vessel at the base of the twenty-mile high structure housing the drive components.

The ridge referenced by Mentar could be seen in the distance on the starboard side of the ship.

Access tunnels, reaching the full twenty-miles to the interior of the ship, were located on all six points of reference to the ship. North, South, East, and West, and then one on each pole of the 900-mile diameter sphere. Each of the tunnels had a sealed door every mile or so. That would be about twenty doors to open and close behind you to enter the ship when it was operational and occupied. The doors were automatic so they would open to let an entering ship pass, then close and seal behind it. By now none of the doors are going to be sealed, however, they would have to be manually cranked open.

Mentar finished relating the technical specifications then turned to the Colonel: "It's not likely that we will find bodies aboard. Apparently the ship was parked here and then, when they discovered that there were planets in the system to accommodate them, they abandoned ship to Solaris 4. Probably choosing it because Solaris 4 was closest to the size and gravity of our home planet. It was probably a long drawn out process to abandon the ship. I would think that there were thousands of them. It would have been multiple trips back and forth considering the size of the ancient ship. No doubt they took all the supplies, food stuffs, plants, tools, seeds, everything needed to start over on Solaris 4. There's probably one tunnel that's open; the one they chose to use in the evacuation. When they shut down the ship for the last time and left with the last load of evacuees and or supplies; there would have been no reason to manually close the doors behind them. It's likely that all the other entrances are still closed for space flight."

"That makes sense," Marvin said. "First order of business is to find that gateway to the interior and to check out the ports for entering the drive. The bounty we seek is likely in and around the drive. Okay," Marvin concluded, "it's early afternoon some 800,000,000 miles away, and since we are operating on Earth time, let's dispatch the shuttles and guppies and locate the entrances we need, then prepare to enter the vessel tomorrow morning. We could all use a little time to acclimate ourselves to this very weak gravity."

Marvin thought for a moment. "Let's configure the guppies for passengers, two of Mentar's people each, say Mentar and Nycron in Guppy 1 and Kronos and Juno in Guppy 2. If they need to leave the ship to check out the entranceways, use tethered suits this time. Shuttlecraft One and Guppy 1, investigate gaining access to the drive components. Shuttlecraft Two and Guppy 2, locate that open gate to the interior of the ship."

One hour later the parties were ready for the assignments and launched. Shuttle One and Guppy 1 approached the twenty-mile-high enclosure then turned left toward the east, the leading edge of Iapetus in its orbit. Shuttle Two and Guppy 2 headed for the point on Iapetus closest to Saturn, a point of the compass declared to be North on a generated reference map.

In less that fifteen minutes, Shuttle One slowed and stopped at an indenture. It was one of the access ports to the drive area. It was closed. The crew could see the mechanism for manually cranking it open. Its dimensions were sized for the giants. J. D., pilot of Shuttle One radioed Discovery: "Colonel, we've located one of the ports to the drive. It has rigging for hand cranking it open."

Mentar added: "Colonel, this is going to be typical all around the drive housing. I'd like to go out and see if this one will crank open after all this time."

"Okay, Mentar, go ahead. We need to know."

"Jake," Mentar said, "set us down next to the port." Mentar and Nycron put on their helmets and pressurized their spacesuits.

Jake landed Guppy 1, depressurized the cargo bay, and opened the doors. Nycron pulled the cover off one of the tether reels and attached the tether to the back of Mentar's pressure suit. Mentar stepped out of the Guppy onto the surface of the ancient spaceship. He took a step toward the cranking mechanism and bounced excessively several feet above the surface. Nycron grabbed his tether and stopped his upward drift. Mentar slowly fell back to the surface. He, very slowly this time, made his way over to the cranking mechanism, carefully anchored himself by holding onto a provided hand-hold, then placed his other hand on the crank. He gently applied pressure clockwise. It began moving smoothly. He, rotating the crank, watched the 70-footby-150-foot double doors move apart from each other leaving a 70-foot-by-300-foot opening. "Colonel," Mentar said, "these doors work just fine. It's the standard opening we've observed everywhere."

"Understood," Marvin replied. "Tomorrow is going to be a busy day. Standby, Shuttle One. Shuttle Two, come in."

"Shuttle Two, go ahead."

"Lucas," Marvin said, "spotted anything."

"Not yet, Sir. Should be soon. Saturn is almost directly overhead. Hold on, I see a blemish on the surface directly ahead."

Two miles farther, a standard 300-by-70 feet indenture on the surface came into view. The gates were closed. The cranking mechanism was visible.

"Colonel," Lucas said, "We found it. The door is closed. It does have a hand opening arrangement; a crank."

"We can go in that way if we have too. However, it would be a difficult. Fly to the leading edge of the sphere relative to Iapetus' orbit and check that one."

"On our way, Sir."

"Shuttle One," Marvin said. "Fly to the trailing edge and check to see if that tunnel is open."

"Will do."

"Colonel," Mentar injected, "the tunnels on the poles, fore and aft, will lead to the center of the rotating cylinder inside that provides artificial gravity. The other four tunnels lead to the storage areas of the interior; the space between the grand cylinder and the outer wall of the craft."

Shuttle Two and Guppy 2 flew to the leading edge of the huge ship, found the door also closed, then ascended to 2000 feet and began the flight back to Discovery. Upon reestablishing line of sight radio contact they reported their findings and continued to the mother ship.

Moments later, Shuttle One called in the sought-after report. The west tunnel, the trailing edge of Iapetus, was open all the way to the core of the vessel.

Again, night fell on Discovery by the clock. Tonight would be very different. Tonight, routine communication with Earth was not possible due to the long wait time for a response. Two and a half hours. The best thing to do was to transmit an informative message of the day's activity in a conclusive form. Wait two and a half hours for a possible reply and call it a day. Tonight, also, would be a night spent sleeping with *Zero-G* restraints fastened. *One-40th-G* was enough gravity to dictate a reclining position, but not enough to keep a person, geared to *one-g*, in place without straps.

Mentar gave an account of the day, knowing the students back on Earth would be waiting anxiously to hear something, then, signed off, and cut the radio link for the day.

Chapter 16

PRECIOUS METALS

Discovery's crew begin to stir as the clock faithfully introduced a new day. The night's rest had been fitful and awkward for most of the crew. The very faint gravity was a challenging reality for all aboard. However, the insatiable curiosity of what lay inside the ancient ship of such enormous size was much more gripping. Following the morning meal, all were tuned in to the organizational meeting outlining the procedure to investigate the ancient vessel.

"First on the agenda," Marvin said, "let's enter the drive compartment, the ridge circling the ship, and recover some of the components that appear to include precious metals; things of value. That's our priority. J.D., ready Guppy 1 with all your equipment for removing components and bringing them aboard. Maggie, Guppy 2 will be a transport for Mentar and his group. Shuttles One and Two will fly escort inside the drive housing."

The respective crews went about arranging their craft for the excursion. When ready to launch, Marvin, Frank, and Doug boarded Shuttle One and Dave and Roger boarded Shuttle Two. The four ships waited for their hangar bays to depressurize and for the doors to open. They exited, formed a formation just outside Discovery, and then, with Guppy 2 in the lead, headed for the first access door, already opened by Mentar.

Upon approaching the door, the group saw an arm of a pressure suit sticking out from behind the newly opened door. It was giant-size. Maggie stopped the ship. "A body?!"

Mentar studied the suit. "No. The suit's empty. It must have been floating loose in the compartment and when I opened the door it drifted to this wall and settled on the door. No doubt, it was part of their emergency equipment. All around the drive there are small rooms with pressurization equipment. If you punctured your suit you cound quickly retreat into the room, pressurize it, then put one of these emergency suits on."

"Let's recover that," Marvin said. "Guppy One, suit up, depressurize, and bring it aboard so we can take it back to Discovery. There will be things to learn from that suit."

Jake and his team recovered the pressure suit that came from Alpha Centauri and secured it in the cargo bay. Then they continued to follow Guppy One as she entered the drive housing. Once inside, Mentar looked up toward the twenty-mile-high pinnacle of the drive structure. Light from the open entrance illuminated the surroundings for several hundred feet, and then the maze of electronics faded into blackness.

"Colonel,' Mentar said, "we are going to need all of the ship's lights combined to view the electronic mountings."

The Armada entered the huge structure housing tons and tons of electronic components, circuit boards, mazes of wiring, and unrecognizable circuitry. They turned to the right, back toward the mothership's location, turned on all ship's lights, and proceeded slowly along the drive. It quickly became evident through the reflection of the lights off the components that the *goods* were there.

The Armada held while Mentar and his group suited up for an excursion. Maggie depressurized the cargo bay of Guppy 2 and opened the doors. Mentar pointed upward and to the left. She slowly flew the guppy in that direction. Ahead was a hundred-foot-square mounting protruding outward from the rest of the wall of electronics. There were twenty or so clusters of interconnected components plugged into the mounting. Mentar, using hand holds, pulled himself to the end of the cargo bay, reached up and began unplugging them and handing them to Kronos who passed them on back to Nycron to be stacked in the cargo bay.

Jim and Dennis, in Guppy 1, suited up. Jake depressurized the cargo bay and opened the doors. They began detaching components and storing them in Guppy 1's cargo bay.

"Colonel," Mentar said, "there are access ports here about fifty-feet-square that go through these electronic mountings. They are pathways that go as far as I can see. One of the shuttles would fit and could get some pictures of this equipment."

"Stand by," Marvin said, then instructed J.D. to move Shuttle 1 alongside Guppy 2. Mentar pointed at the access tunnel. J.D. steered Shuttle One into it.

As Marvin watched the components pass by the ship, he felt like a miniature person flying through the back of an old-fashioned battery-powered radio, with its cathode ray tubes, transformers, and ancient wiring. The number of electronic mountings, wiring, and unknown components was overwhelming. "I might be wrong," Marvin said into the radio, "but I get the impression that these electronics reflect the early technology of your people, Mentar. Probably, a modern day component, even like we now have on Earth, the size of a postage stamp, would do the same job as a square yard of these components. That's why there's so much precious metals used here."

Doug checked to make sure the camera was on line and getting everything.

"To build this vessel," Marvin said, "then board it, and head out among the stars was a bold venture indeed. There must have been a pressing reason to do it."

Shuttle One exited the access way and rejoined the Armada.

"Colonel," Mentar said, "according to the research library these electronics circle the starship completely to generate a propulsion field.

"Understood," Marvin said. "Looks like there's every bit of the metals you promised the president, and then some, here for salvaging. Go ahead and remove enough of the components to fill the two containers to return to Earth. Look for and remove several different components for a good sampling of what's here. Before we return to Discovery and prepare to enter the interior of the ship, I want to fly a few miles around this equatorial ridge and see if these electronics repeat. Are the clusters different all the way around the vessel or do they repeat every so often?"

When Mentar and company completed filling the guppy's cargo bays to capacity, the Armada began a flight along the electronic compartments around the curving structure. Soon, Marvin's question was answered. They saw repetition less than a mile ahead. The electronics were mounted in segments; a giant version of the patterns that were used on earth in building electric motors, where the magnets were spaced around an armature that when energized would cause the motor to spin. Here, when energized, the field caused the ship to move in a selected direction. This would be a serious challenge of reverse engineering, indeed.

The Armada returned to Discovery. The two guppies made another trip to the drive housing to recovery additional components to fill the crates supplied by NASA.

Marvin, satisfied that the president's directive had been accomplished, elected to move Discovery to the access tunnel that was open, on the trailing edge of Iapetus, some 600 miles away. All excursion craft were moored and personnel notified. Discovery rose from the surface and proceeded to fly to the open tunnel.

She was landed and 'anchored' for the exploration of the interior of the ancient ship.

Marvin, perhaps in a bit of a political move, assigned all 14 of the guests from around the world places on the six excursion craft that were about to enter the ancient spaceship. A total of 42 from Discovery would be aboard the Armada; 6 on each shuttle, 6 of the guests and the 4 giants aboard Guppy 1 plus its crew of 4, and Guppy 2's crew of 4. The cargo bay on Guppy 2 would be empty, pending recovering something deemed valuable to return to Earth.

The excursion team, reminded by Marvin, knew that the farther they descended into the starship orbiting Saturn, the lower the tug of gravity would be. It would creep toward zero as they approached the center of mass of the vessel. That fact did not deter their motivation to go and see the extraterrestrial craft for themselves.

DAN HOLT

Chapter 17

THE INTERIOR

Shuttle One entered the tunnel, passing the first set of open double doors, and then proceeded slowly with it lights searching ahead. As they progressed, the crew noticed that on each side of the ship, every hundred feet or so, there was a port hole about six feet across on both sides of the tunnel. On the other side of the transparent round window there was a mixture of soil and rocks. Marvin signaled the Armada, then slowly brought Shuttle One to a stop at one of the windows and examined it closely, then moved to the next one and studied it. "It looks like this ship was a moon of their home planet and they hollowed it out for use as a transport between the stars."

"Actually," Jakov Ivanski, the Russian Cosmonaut joined in, "that's pretty smart. Look how cratered the surface of the ship, or, moon is. Think what that would do to a manufactured surface of a ship."

"There would be some blemishes alright," Marvin said, "however, I think most of those craters on

173

the surface were done after the ship parked here in Saturn orbit. When Solaris 4 exploded."

"No doubt," Ivanski agreed, "but you can be sure that some of them happened during that four and a half lightyear transit from there to here."

Shuttle One and the Armada resumed the twenty-mile trek through the outer hull of the ship. The first mile passed, and soon gate 2 passed by the ships. "Nineteen miles to go," Maggie said, flying directly behind Shuttle One.

The crews were silent for some time as the doors, marking the miles, passed by in silence and absolute stillness. Mile 5 passed, then 10. It seemed the throat of the beast went on forever. Mile 15, then 18. Dave blinked several times, leaned forward, and studied the tunnel through the windshield. "Colonel," he said excitedly, "it looks like there's a glow ahead!" Marvin studied the tunnel in the distance. "All ships, turn off your lights for a moment." All the lights winked out and total darkness surrounded the Armada. The crews slowly became aware of a glow ahead as their eyes adjusted to the darkness.

"Okay," Marvin said. "Lights on. It looks like the interior of the ship is lighted. Perhaps we got lucky and this vessel is also rigged with Solar Mechanical or Starlight Mechanical lighting."

Doug observed: "If this ship runs on starlight it could run forever and go anywhere; that is, if the drive is in order."

Dave added: "That would probably indicate that the ship is not very fast; starlight if very weak, but is always there. No doubt the ship had unlimited range. Their journey this far may have taken many years if not a couple of centuries."

"Mentar," Marvin said. "Have you found any information about the ship's power source?"

"Not yet, Colonel. I'll be looking for that information in the reference library."

The Armada resumed forward motion to traverse the last two miles to the interior and all that was waiting. When they passed the last set of airlock doors there was a set of the same-sized doors on the right wall of the tunnel. They were equipped with the cranking mechanism as on the ports of the drive housing. Marvin noted as the ships cruised by: "We'll check out what's behind those doors later."

The light ahead, now less than a quarter of a mile away, grew gradually brighter as they approached, but still dimly lighted compared to the brilliant system encountered on the Moon. Here, much farther from the energy supplying star, the light had to be greatly amplified to yield the lumens they were witnessing.

Minutes later the Armada exited the tunnel into an immense volume of open space. Dead ahead, five hundred yards away, was a giant tube, at least a quarter mile across, that extended out of sight toward the other side of the ship. It was like looking directly at the end of a soda straw. Coming from the wall of the craft at a 45-degree angle to the central tube were shafts or braces, four of them, that were holding the quarter-mile tube in place. It was the substructure holding the giant axle for the rotating drum; the mechanism to supply artificial gravity.

It was the suspended rotating drum Mentar had mentioned, 400 miles wide and 400 miles in diameter. The edge of the cylinder, on this side, would be about 200 miles away, straight down the axis. It was so far away that the naked eye could only distinguish varying shades of gray on its surface. The overall shape was clearly distinguishable from this central vantage point. They could see directly into the hollow tube and saw that it was also home to electronic components appearing similar to those encountered in the drive. No doubt, they were the circuitry for the central lights or *suns* to light the giant cylinder. All around the central mechanism, extending inward from the outer hull of the spacecraft, were the stationary parts of the ship; cubicles, rooms, enclosures, apparently intended for storage of supplies. All of them were empty save for a few with a loose item or two still remaining on the floors or walls where the microgravity had allowed them to settle. Marvin, staring at the scene, said, "This ship would carry enough furniture to stock a planet."

"Apparently, it did just that," Ivanski agreed.

No details of the artificial gravity system could be seen at that great a distance. Marvin imagined the giant cylinder slowly and majestically rotating as its thousands of occupants went about their daily routines. The dimensions were so enormous it would seem to them that they were standing on a planet instead of being enclosed in a hollowed out moon.

"Let's go have a close look," Marvin said. "Everybody stay alert."

J.D. eased the ship forward, flew upward to clear the huge axle, and then began the trek to the near side of the giant cylinder. They flew along the axis of the cylinder, making their way toward the center. The miles rolled by. The overwhelming size of the ship made the Armada seem like insects buzzing around new territory, hoping for a reward.

The size of the world around them made their 400-plus miles per hour velocity seem slow indeed. Soon, the near side of the rotating drum came into view. There were huge pods, football shaped, clustered around the mounting of the central cylinder, four of them, sticking out from the side wall of the enormous drum.

"Those look like the booster units in your rotor pods, Frank," Doug said. "How about that."

"Yeah, I see that. It looks like the mounting of the huge cylinder onto the shaft is a magnetic arrangement. There's no actual contact with the shaft. That would give it virtually zero drag or resistance."

"J.D.," Marvin said. "Let's fly toward the outer hull of the ship and locate an access to get inside the cylinder where the living quarters were."

Shuttle One and the Armada began a transit outward from the central shaft of the rotating cylinder arrangement of the vessel. Several miles outward of the axis they came to an open view of inside the living area of the ship. At this point the cylinder had spokes extending to the outer solid surface; the perimeter of the cylinder. The Armada turned and flew between the spokes and into the giant cylinder.

Below were the housing areas, the parks, the countryside, the cultivated fields, the forest and then the prairie, now abandoned and derelict, all quiet and still. The slightest touch to any of it would likely result in it turning to dust to wander the confines of the ship until it found a place to settle. The good ship, Iapetus, may well have been here, silent, for a quarter-million years. The Armada began a descent to the surface below.

Doug, sitting on a fold-down bench behind the copilot on Shuttle One, pulled on his lap belt a little tighter to counter his body drifting from the seat. He was studying the joints in the cylinder wall as they descended. It was made up of hundreds of thousands of rectangle-shaped segments that were small enough that they would pass through the entrance tunnel. "Just think," he said, "all of this, the entire mechanism, was brought in through the tunnel we entered. It's staggering to think about the number of trips it took to complete the ship."

"Maybe the pieces interlocked together," Frank said, "like a puzzle and they figured out how to bring in a hundred at a time."

"It was a major effort," Marvin joined. "If there was a constant stream through all the tunnels at once, it would take months just to assemble this cylinder. They were determined."

They approached the floor of the cylinder below. Marvin noticed that Mentar had been silent for some time. "Mentar, you okay?"

"Yes, Colonel. I was just thinking. All this seems so remote. So far removed. It's like I am exploring some other race's gallant effort to go to the stars."

"It is a very long step back into the past."

"I'd like to know why they left the Alpha Centauri system. This ship is not as advanced as I expected. It's as if they were willing to take a chance on it actually getting them there. It indicates to me that they had no alternative but to leave the star system."

"Maybe the answer is in some of the materials you are researching," Marvin offered. "If you and your people are going back there, be sure there's a home waiting."

Chapter 18

THE SURFACE

The eight ships sat on the surface of the cylinder inside the ancient starship, in a semicircle facing an enormous box-shaped structure. The building had no roof. On the descent, square shapes were seen inside it.

"Tethered?" someone asked as multiple crewmembers began suiting up in their respective craft.

"I think we have enough redundancy here," Marvin said. "Untethered is okay. Anyone gets in trouble, don't wait, sound off. Don't forget to take one of the personal thrusters. One wrong move and you could drift for miles up into this artificial sky. All crewmembers set your radio's on *KEY TRANSMIT AUTO RECEIVE*. We don't want multiple communications overlapping to confuse a real problem. Then select an alternate frequency for your immediate team. It will be live, so when you key you will be received by everybody."

When the four giants were helmeted in their pressure suits and checked out, Jake opened the outer doors of the cargo bay. He heard the faint whine of the twin rotor pods countering the inertial mass of the doors movement; keeping the guppy in place. Mentar, Kronos, Nycron, and Brock exited the guppy and stood up and surveyed the work of their ancient ancestors. In looking around it seemed that the fact that they were here, now, alive, was indeed a miracle. And, Mentar was contemplating taking just as bold a chance of returning home. However, he felt that he had better equipment and a better chance at success. With at least this much luck they would get home safe and sound to send a special message to the Little Ones. The Little Ones would have to wait four and a half years to receive the signal; however, they would have already been waiting for 22 years during the ships transit time.

Mentar, with his hand thruster at the ready, lead the way toward the nearest structure.

Marvin watched Mentar walk by Shuttle One in soft bouncing steps. He would take a step, then fire a very short burst from his thruster over his shoulder and drift slowly back to the surface while advancing forward. Apparently he had years of experience and many episodes of weightlessness to his credit. Marvin exited his ship and, using the same technique, followed

Mentar and his colleagues into the structure. The others must have been watching and taking notes. Soon, there were a dozen more of the crewmembers making their way into the structure, each sporting a thruster.

Mentar looked up toward the top of the wall of the spacious enclosure. There was a platform about 200 feet up with a single circular leg, about seventy feet in diameter, under its center. Inside it were stairs spiraling upward. The platform was 500-feet square. Marvin glanced around the structure. There were several more duplicates scattered around the room.

"Mentar," Marvin said, "why are they suspended above the floor?"

"I don't know," Mentar responded. "Perhaps they used this space on the floor for other things. That is curious. Let's see what's up there."

Mentar headed for the stairwell in the column. He entered and began the climb. He effortlessly traversed the distance and stepped over to the edge of the platform, waved at the explorers below and then disappeared. A moment later, he reappeared at the edge of the platform and signaled for the others to come up. They bounced over to the column and began the ascent in single file, using the thrusters combined with pulling themselves upward. Soon they were all on the suspended floor. There was an assortment of desks and chairs, giant-size, scattered around the platform. The arrangement gave the impression of a library setting. Mentar handed Marvin a crystalline disc with a cluster on a pedestal mounted in the center of it. It resembled the ones found on the moon with the exception that the pedestals were shorter and the crystalline clusters were wider in diameter.

Marvin's and Mentar's eyes met. Marvin looked up at the top of the desk and triggered his thruster and guided himself upon the desktop. He reached into an open box and picked up another disc. "Mentar, these are going to be about your home!"

"I know," Mentar responded. "This place was here before the lab on the Moon existed."

"Is there a projection machine?"

Mentar pointed toward the other end of the desk. "It's dead; everything here is, except the Solar Mechanical lights and they're very dim."

"Let's take them back to Discovery and power them."

Mentar nodded and picked up the machine. His colleagues scouted the platform and gathered all the crystalline discs and machines.

"Maggie," Marvin said into the radio, "bring Guppy 2 close to the door and open the cargo bay. We have some goodies for you."

Mentar, Kronos, Nycron, and Brock located and loaded on the guppy four machines and some thirty-seven discs with various configurations of crystalline clusters.

While they were checking all the platforms for more of the precious finds, the two Japanese specialists, Akio Aihara and Namiko Abe, made their way back to the floor and were going door-to-door of the many rooms in the structure hoping to find left-behind computers; something really intriguing to study. They traversed the full width of the building with no results. Rounding a corner of the building, they spotted another raised platform. They informed Marvin, received approval, and entered the stairwell and ascended to the top of the raised floor. On the far side of the platform, near the edge, there were two boxes about six feet square. Curiosity took them straight to them. Together they raised the lid to full-open on the nearest one.

Attempting to look inside, Akio jumped and fired his thruster at the same time, mistakenly giving himself excessive velocity. He grabbed the side of the box to stop himself. The action flipped him over the edge of the box, kicking his legs outward. They hit Namiko in the chest, boosting him toward the sky at about 10 feet per second velocity. Surprised by the blow to his chest, he lost his grip on his thruster, losing it in the process. He quickly gained a hundred feet altitude and was still climbing. He keyed his radio and sounded off a warning. "Colonel, I'm drifting away from the floor fast! I've lost my thruster and can't stop myself."

"Jake..." Marvin said.

"I see him, Colonel. I'll get him."

Jake, with his cargo bay doors already open, rose from the floor, lined up his ship with the tumbling figure, and began movement toward him, increasing his speed gradually, ready to match the programmer's speed to avoid injuring him. He caught up with him about a half mile above the surface, eased forward closing the gap slowly until Namiko was tumbling in the mouth of the cargo bay. Namiko was able to grasp a hand hold and counter his tumbling motion. Jake brought the guppy to a stop. He held for a moment to allow Namiko's rotational energy to dissipate and the Japanese A.I. programmer to collect himself. He then turned around and headed back to the floor a half-mile below. He eased the guppy up to the platform and allowed Namiko to exit on the platform where he had been launched into the sky. Namiko turned toward Jake and bowed then spoke in perfect English: "I'm glad you were here today, Mr. Jake." Jake gave him a nod, then returned to his parking place, and landed his ship.

Akio, realizing his mistake had launched his colleague skyward, saw the guppy responding to the mishap. He looked around for Namiko's thruster. It was drifting across the platform toward the opening to the support column. Using his own, he followed and retrieved it, then returned to the position next to the crate. He watched as the guppy turned and began the return to the platform. Namiko was standing in the entrance way to the guppy's cargo bay, holding on to two of the hand holds, facing the direction of travel like a captain standing on the bow of his ship eyeing an objective. Somehow, it didn't seem out of character. Soon, the guppy eased up to the platform graciously and came to a stop. Namiko stepped out onto the platform. Then, when the guppy pulled away, Akio handed his thruster unit to him.

They, using appropriate caution, again pulled themselves up and looked in the box. Inside were two or three dozen bowls about three feet across, some of them two feet deep and others about a foot deep. Some of the stacks had pieces broken out of the sides of them. Akio reached down and picked up one of them. It was about an inch in thickness. He looked at Namiko. "What do you think they are?"

"A set of dishes," Namiko answered. "Some are broken so they left them behind."

"That raises questions," Akio said, "where did they prepare food; cook and serve? Where's the kitchen, the cafeteria, tables, chairs, and all the stuff that goes with it?"

They both began searching into the distance toward the horizon. In this case, the horizon curved upward instead of dropping away out of sight. The distance was so great that detail could not be seen with the naked eye.

The treasures found were loaded into Guppy 2, then the crews began returning to the Armada to fly farther around the circumference of the rotating-part of the ship. The eight ships, flying abreast, began a slow flight toward the rising horizon, gradually increasing speed as the miles rolled by. They were flying across an enormous field that was obviously used for growth of plant life, food or oxygen-making flora, or both.

"Colonel," Alexia Mulinkov, the extended space flight researcher from Russia, said, "I'd like to know what kind of soil they used for growing their food and other plants. Could we get a sample of it so I can study it?"

"Alexia?"

"Yes, Sir."

"Standby."

Marvin slowed the Armada momentarily and dipped down close to the surface to see if there was indeed soil spread on the surface. He discovered that the entire surface of the field was individual pots of soil or some artificial medium that served as soil. Alexia saw the individual pots sitting in rows with walking room only between the rows. "Oh yes! Get me one of those pots!"

Marvin smiled. "Make that two. Jake, have Jim, Dennis, and Zeke go out and get two of them and load them in Guppy 2's cargo bay."

Jake cruised to the nearest access aisle, landed the guppy, and opened the doors for the suited team. Maggie joined him on the floor with an open cargo bay. An up-close visual revealed their true size. The pots were ten-feet across and six-feet deep. The crew moved all of the bounty recovered on the raised platform to the back of the open cargo bay and brought in two of the pots. The collective load filled half the cargo bay. They returned to their ship. Maggie closed the doors and the guppies returned to a matching altitude with the Armada. Marvin resumed forward flight.

As the miles rolled by, the skyline of multiple buildings, about ten miles in the distance, began to take shape. Dave scanned across the horizon again. "A city?"

"There are buildings that are duplicated several times." Doug said. "It could be a factory or processing plant of some type. The food grown here would have to be prepared for consumption."

Soon, the Armada was flying over the cluster of buildings. There were four or five different building-designs that were duplicated several times. Maybe it was a processing area or, perhaps, a dining area for the occupants of the enormous ship.

"I've got a hunch," Marvin said. "Let's fly toward the center of the farm. It's going to be about 200 miles, if I'm right."

The Armada turned right and began a trek toward the center of the huge, once-rotating, cylindrical structure. Colonel Ivanski turned and looked at Marvin. "You expect to find water."

"Yes; well, no. The water won't be there now but the evidence of it will be. The banks of a river, lake, or a sea. It takes lots of water to grow food and also to sustain thousands of residents."

Minutes later as the distance was reduced the crew could barely make out twin walls, built about five miles apart, running parallel to each other, circling the entire 400-mile diameter cylinder. They looked like smooth walls about a quarter-mile high. Soon, the

Armada approached the nearest one. It was constructed of the same rectangular shapes as the cylinder itself. Marvin ascended to the top to see what was on the other side.

An expansive valley came into view. Its bottom was well below the surface level of the rest of the cylinder. It looked like a river bed or lake bottom. It circled the entire *world* as well.

"It looks like they maintained a water level in this that was well above the living areas and the fields," Marvin said. "That would act as the water towers do in neighborhoods on Earth. It would give them water pressure wherever they needed it."

The Armada began a descent down into the lake bed. About a hundred feet below the bottom of the wall there were pipes, about thirty feet in diameter, leading away from the waterway at a ninety-degree angle. They were imbedded into the lake bottom. "Water supply lines," Doug said, "taking water to the towns, living areas, food prepping station, and, no doubt, irrigation for the farms, forests, and prairies. This ship was a flying world."

"We need more information," Brock, the historian and counselor to the giants said, "on how they did this. This ship could not have been launched from the surface of a planet. It had to have been built in space, in orbit."

"How would they make hundreds of thousands of trips to and from orbit," Dave said. That's not reasonable."

Marvin looked at the ship's chronometer then addressed the Armada: "Let's return to Discovery and a night's rest. We'll return here tomorrow and resume our search. We'll focus on locating a library; a records-keeping area.

With all the ships moored in Discovery, maintenance collected all the pressure suits for inspection and servicing of the air tanks. When the crews settled down to the *comforts of home* and the faint gravity, they began to experience fatigue and hunger. They headed for the lounges and conversation about their day. The exploration of a ship created by an amazingly gallant civilization that took a very bold step out into the cosmic sea of stars.

Tomorrow they would search further for records of how they did it and, perhaps, why.

Chapter 19

BORN

The White House

President Howell, settled in at his desk for a trying day of contacting various nations regarding the up-and-coming business of building a starship. Momentarily, the phone rang. He picked it up. He was being connected to his liaison to the giants; Dwight Cummins. "Mr. President, I'm at the clinic, in the waiting room, at Giant City."

Walter Howell's pulse went up; this was going to be a more gripping day still. "Go ahead, Dwight."

"Milan was just brought in, checked by her doctors, the four in medical school, then taken to delivery waiting. She's in labor. The medical students brought two of their instructors will them to monitor their handling of their first case. They seem quite confident."

"Okay, keep me informed. Let me know when the baby arrives."

"Yes, Sir."

President Howell hung up the phone. Now, back to the business at hand. He'd spent the last few days visiting, by phone, with various nations that were predicted to be of a posture to get involved in the construction of a starship for the giants to leave Earth and return to their home some four and a half lightyears away. All of them, without exception, wanted a face-to-face meeting with Mentar and his colleagues. Understandable. A project of such magnitude is a serious and very expensive thing. However, the compensation was ample; awkward, but ample. It was a new, and in some respects, scary world. It would give birth to many new companies. It would better the world economies while complicating them as well.

Over the past two years or so articles had popped up in different magazines, newspapers, and science journals; about think-tanks and engineering groups who had proposed various designs of ships to set sail for the stars using the propulsion system that came out of a Chicago inventor's lab. Now, it appeared that all those designs will, at least, get a viewing. Perhaps a combination of all the proposals would produce a winner. The ship must take care of 1216 of the adult giants and, perhaps, as many as a dozen children or perhaps more by the time the craft was completed, tested, and finally launched to the stars.

Dwight, the president's liaison, had talked at length with Meta and Mingee, the attending Counselors at Giant City, about the premise of constructing the ship and outfitting it for the journey. They had mentioned that they would have to return to the Moon and get some of their equipment that was being used there during their tenure in service to the elderly. They had mentioned growing-pots for certain foods among other things.

Further, before the giants left the Solar System to return home, they wanted to pay their personal respects and set up a tribute, a permanent marker to the 400 students and two Counselors that did not survive.

Walter Howell read the latest report from Saturn; reading and re-reading the description of the enormous scale of the vessel that the original giants had managed to construct, launch, and reach the Solar System. Whether it was their intended destination or not; it was a miraculous accomplishment. Soon, probably in the next generation, Earth would be players in that arena. What an adventure-filled future!

Dwight Cummins had brought news of two more pregnancies at Giant City, Kansas. And, now, today the first pregnancy had run its course and the birth was imminent. No sooner than the thought had settled in the mind, the phone rang.

"Five feet, four inches; eighty-two pounds, six and a half ounces. Aledo Mentar Kaavienne. Everybody's okay. By the way, you can add three more pregnancies to the list according to Mingee."

"Dwight, we have a ship to build."

Chapter 20

SEARCHING

Onboard Discovery – Saturn System

Alexia Mulinkov, having dinner with her fellow Russian colleague, Colonel Jakov Ivanski, and two of his recent acquaintances, Ammon Tacitus and Kago Tebogo, of the fledgling South African Space Agency, got involved in a deep conversation with the South African representatives concerning their Agency. The two formative members of the African effort had sought out Colonel Ivanski. They were full of questions about the particulars of approaching the spacefaring business.

The African Agency had promise, she thought, if these representative's efforts were endorsed by the nation they served. They were sincere, honest, and dedicated.

Communications Room - Discovery

The receiving equipment came alive for several seconds, then went quiet. The tape dispensed forward three inches and then was cut off. Robert Sheridan pulled it from the machine and read it. He smiled, folded it once, then handed it to an assistant. "Mentar, Deck 4." The courier headed up the stairs, entered the land of the giants, located Mentar and handed him the memo, then headed back to the communications room. Mentar opened the note and looked at it. It read: *Aledo Mentar Kaavienne. Born Planet Earth. Five feet four inches; eighty-two pounds six and a half ounces. Mother and baby are fine.*

The buzz of the news began to spread through the ship. It reached the Bridge. Marvin went up the stairs to congratulate Mentar and he fellows. When he reached the head of the stairs, Mentar handed him the memo. Marvin read it then looked up at Mentar. "Congratulations, I see he's named after you."

Mentar nodded and smiled. "I'm honored."

Marvin looked at the memo again. "I notice that there's a last name listed; Kaavienne. I've never asked, Mentar. What's your last name?"

"Kaavienne. However, it's not a name; it's an identity. It means *a child of two Suns*. Everyone has that, so called, last name."

As the evening wore on, Alexia's mind went to the pots of soil from another star, sitting in the cargo bay of Discovery. She excused herself, stepped to one of the consoles and keyed the intercom: "Colonel Andrews, this is Alexia."

"Go ahead."

"Colonel, I would like to take a sample of the soil from one of the pots we recovered today in the starship, take it to the research lab, and take a look."

"Granted, Alexia. Take the precaution of having, at least, two other persons present."

"Will do. Karen and Jean, please come to the research lab."

Alexia picked up a stainless steel sample container from the lab's stores, nodded to the girls, and the three of them crossed the main deck and entered the elevator to the Deck 4. When they exited it, Mentar, having heard Alexia's exchange, was standing there. He pointed to the left. Alexia looked up at him. His profile reminded her of the fabled Colossus of Rhodes. Mentar had stately, chiseled, features. She'd never really looked at him before. She shook of the thought.

The three walked across the cargo bay and approached the two ten-foot-diameter pots. The side walls of the pots were just above their heads. Karen turned and spoke: "Mentar, come here."

Mentar complied. Alexia handed him the sample container. "Get me a sample of the soil in this pot."

Mentar reached down into the pot with the sample container. When it touched the surface of the soil it became apparent that the top of the soil had solidified. Mentar, using his center knuckle, broke the shell of solidification, and filled the stainless steel container with the soil and handed it to Alexia. Alexia gripped the prize with both hands and headed for the elevator. Karen and Jean looked at each other and followed.

In the lab, Alexia took a sample of the soil and put it under the microscope, adjusted it, then peered into the eyepiece. She raised up, looked at the others: "soil is soil in any star system."

Karen viewed the sample through the eyepiece; then Jean did the same.

Alexia took another look, varying the focus. "Wait a minute," she said, fine tuning the focus. "Look at this!"

Karen again peered through the eyepiece. There were precise square cubes of some type of material included in the sample. The cubes were scattered sparsely through the soil. Jean took a look and witnessed the same.

"What ingredient consists of perfect squares?" Alexia said.

"I don't know," Karen and Jean echoed.

Suddenly, Karen caught her breath. "Kronos worked with these type pots, growing food, on the Moon. He would know what it is. Alexia, print out a picture of the sample, highlighting the particle, and let's go talk to him."

Kronos was dictating into the radio recording, for transmission to Earth, an account of the day's activities inside the ancient starship. Alexia, Karen, and Jean waited until he finished his report and responded to them. It was obvious by his demeanor that Kronos, under the direction and influence of Mentar, had grown from a boy to a man. He wanted to know how he could help. Alexia handed him the photograph of the strange particle.

Kronos examined the picture then looked up. "Where did you get this?"

"We examined the soil from the growing-pots we picked up today; the ones from your ancient home; Alpha Centauri, and found that mixed in with it."

Kronos nodded. "This is a growth additive. We used it on the Moon. It makes the hybisfrond plant yield tubers, something like your potatoes, every eight weeks."

"Where does it come from—what is the source?" Alexia asked.

"It came to us on the Moon already processed, ready to use. It was grown on Mars inside the pyramids, in the dark. It looks very similar to your mushroom plants. Our scientists say it's the red soil that does it."

"Oh my God," Alexia said, "What a find! We've got to get an atmosphere on Mars, or what's in that red soil back to Earth."

"An Arcology could be constructed on Mars," Karen said.

"Like the one that was on the Moon," Jean echoed.

"Another new company," Karen continued. "Magic cubes, Inc."

Alexia looked up at Karen and Jean. "You are Americans, that's for sure."

Kronos approached Mentar and related the results of the soil sample test. "Apparently, there's a Mars-like planet in our system; Alpha Centauri. Or, our home planet is the one with red soil.

Mentar made a mental note to be alert for any references in the writings to red soil and special food-growing additives.

The clock dictated that morning of Day 2 had arrived in the Saturn system. The noticed sounded throughout Discovery and hundreds of restraining straps were released as the ship's company began their day. The fact that the crewmembers had been away from the cradle of Earth for 36 days and away from the stabilizing tug of *one-g* for two days, began to be noticed. The permanent signatures of Earth were missed.

Today, the focus of the Armada would be to find whatever records might be on board the ancient ship. Mentar needed all the information available about their home planet in the Alpha Centauri system. The planned venture was bold indeed. Just to know there was a place to live waiting for them was crucial. Even if it was totally undeveloped; it would be a place to start, a place to build on. A home. One of Gulliver's islands. There, they would be normal sentient beings, or giants, or little ones, depending to who came calling.

Marvin went straight to the bridge, as he did every morning for a report on ship's status. Today, from the ship, there was a magnificent view of Saturn with its rings arching across the field of view through the windshield. It triggered some memories in Marvin. During adolescence, he'd eagerly read about the exploits of Commando Cody, a hero from the fifties, checking out the universe in his rocket ship. Commando Cody never seemed to have a fuel problem. However, since then, in the real world, millions of tons of fuel had been expended reaching for space and what might be out there. Millions of tons, until an inventor from Chicago, with the perseverance of a Thomas Edison, experienced a breakthrough and changed everything. The rotor pod required diligent maintenance as does all high-rpm equipment, but no fuel.

Marvin enjoyed the scene of Saturn and its family of moons for moments, then headed for the aft lounge and breakfast.

Mentar read the last communication from Giant City, Kansas. Three more pregnancies. The four students that the president had enrolled in medical school were progressing exceptionally well. They had delivered their first baby and had received an 'A' for their handling of the medical procedures. *"We'll be taking four doctors back home with us,"* Mentar thought.

Mentar's mind went to the interior of the huge vessel they would soon be entering again. Somewhere in that huge contained-space there was information; information he needed. There was a total of half-a-million square-miles of living area inside that enormous cylinder. They would have to search only the areas likely to include records. And, much of that will be guesswork.

He would talk to the Colonel. Today they needed to search for schools; places of instruction. This ship was a long-duration vessel. The young would have to be schooled. They would be taught history. Perhaps in those teaching aids would be the information he needed.

The Armada, restocked, and its crews, better able to handle the faint gravity, entered the long straight tunnel to the interior of Iapetus. Marvin and Mentar had discussed a plan to better the chances of locating some critical information. It was considered an educated guess that a building designated for instruction of the young would be single story, larger that the adjacent buildings, and have greater space around it. At any rate, it was a start on trying to reconcile the enormous area of the starship to be covered and the allocated time for the Mission.

Upon approaching the central axis in the interior, the Armada went to the right of the giant tube and proceeded to a location on the outer rim of the cylinder, one-hundred-eighty degrees from the area probed the day before. Upon arrival at the living surface, they fanned out and began combing the surface dwellings, passing over fields and prairies, then more dwellings. Half an hour went by, then the first prospect was spotted. The Armada settled on the spacious *yard* of the structure.

In half an hour, the crews began exiting their craft and heading for the entrance. All had learned to use their thrusters fairly well and moved efficiently into the building entrance. It was a hallway at the end of which was a set of double doors; closed. Mentar, approached them, grasped the two handles and pulled the fifty-foot doors open. Inside was a vast space of empty floor. Apparently, the contents were removed, leaving only a few odds and ends. The crew spotted several containers, barrel-shaped in one of the back corners of the structure. They headed for them out of curiosity. There was writing on the side of each of them; a cluster of circles and triangles.

"Mentar," Marvin said, "what does that say?"

"Spice," Mentar responded, then picked up another and read it. It was the same. He set the drum down, released the lid, and lifted it off the container.

The drum was half-empty. The contents were caked and dried out, powdery in texture. "These containers had been opened so they left them when they evacuated the ship."

"They thought of everything," Doug commented. "When they set sail, they had their spices with them to flavor their foods."

"Smart," Brock, Mentar's colleague said. "We have to think of everything as well. Once we leave, what we have with us will be it until arrival plus however long it takes to build an infrastructure.

The crews returned to their ships and resumed the search. As the miles rolled by they passed over another duplicate of the previous structure. Then, to the right, near the walls that controlled the water system, there was a building, long and narrow, with a larger yard on either end of it.

"Maybe," Marvin said. "It's worth a look."

Mentar agreed and the ships, again, landed in the yard and went about disembarking and entering the structure. The doors were open and they saw a sea of chairs, half giant size, all facing a raised platform with three desk-and-chair arrangements on it, spaced evenly across the platform.

"This is it," Mentar said with enthusiasm. "Hopefully, we'll find some materials here."

"Why would they leave this behind?" Dave asked to no one in particular.

"Much bulk, little value," Mentar responded. "That would be my guess. Look at the chairs. They are very plain. Also, notice the empty frames behind the instructor's platform. They did take the projection monitors. Let's check all the storage rooms and cabinets and see if any printed material was left."

The various crews began a detailed search of the building. A few of the searchers got physical reminders to move slowly and carefully, having to counter their self-imposed launch from the floor with their provided thrusters.

"Over here," came from Colonel Ivanski. He came out of a small room with a two-by-six-foot box about two feet deep. He noticed its inertial resistance when he tried to walk with it. It had considerable mass. Had there been more gravity present in the building, there would have been considerable weight.

Mentar picked up the box, took it to the platform at the front of the room and opened it. The inside was filled with reading-machine-sized books. They were all the same. There were twenty-four per layer and the box was near full. Mentar picked up one of them and read the print on the cover then turned toward Marvin. "It says: **The two Suns of Zannia, a**

Study in Agriculture! They're what you would call textbooks!"

Brock, Kronos, and Nycron each grabbed a copy, opened it and began reading. Mentar read a little on the first page, then looked up and the two dozen fellow explorers standing around them. "Zannia's the name of our home planet!" he said, then continued to read.

Marvin nodded. He paused a moment, then looked from giant-to-giant. They were all immersed in their books, reading. He cleared his throat, noticeably. Mentar stopped reading, glanced around at the group again, then addressed his fellow giants. "Okay, let's put the books back in the box. We can read them tonight back in the ship."

The giants reluctantly put the books back, stacking them neatly, and closed it.

"Colonel! Mentar!" sounded in everyone's helmet. "Come look at this!" Akio and Namiko had made their way across the room through the maze of desks to a cubicle about fifty feet square. They were pointing upward toward the top of the enclosure. Moments later the group had gathered around it. "There," Akio said, pointing to a huge book about seven feet high, five feet wide and about a foot thick. Mentar quickly picked it up, turned it upright and read the Title on the front of it: *"The Building of Zannia 2, Second*

Edition." He turned it over. One the back was a picture of a red planet with a space elevator reaching into the heavens, and hovering near the top of the four-sided latticework tower, was Iapetus, the moon surrounding them at this moment.

Marvin looked from the image on the back of the huge book to Mentar's face. "I guess you have your answer about your home planet."

Mentar handed the book to Brock. He looked at the image a long time then laid his hand on it and rubbed it with his fingertips, then handed it to Kronos and Nycorn. They spoke briefly in Moon. Mentar glanced at them. "English."

Kronos paused a moment. "Mentar, do you think the space elevator is still there?"

"We are going to find out."

The Armada returned to Discovery for a meal and the servicing of the pressure suits and all excursion craft. Also, maintenance wanted to check all the hand thrusters. Mentar addressed the Colonel. "We have not seen the Command Center of this starship. I don't think it's in the gravity hub. I believe it's going to be in the protective shell where the drive itself is housed."

"Probably those doors we passed entering the ship," Marvin agreed, "the one's right after the last pressure gate. Let's take a two-hour break and go check it out. Four ships will be enough; two shuttles and the two guppies."

"I want to try to locate their navigation computer," Mentar continued, "and charts of the checkpoints they used to get here. On that training bridge on Mars it was indicated that there were star charts in their navigation equipment when I experimented with the mockup controls. That could be helpful. There may be some valuable information on what to expect when we get in the vicinity of the Centauri system."

"Make's sense," Marvin said.

DAN HOLT

Chapter 21

COMMAND CENTRAL

Aboard Discovery

Mentar, completing a five-minute broadcast, sent it on its way toward the heart of the Solar System, to Giant City, Kansas. The giants now living on Earth would know, for the first time, the name of their home planet. To Mentar, the name Zannia had a musical ring to it. He had spent thirty minutes eating lunch and then began reading a copy of a book from the find. Brock, Kronos, and Nycron had done the same.

Karen went to Deck 4 and picked up a copy to take to the linguist lab and translate to English.

The White House

President Walter Howell read his copy of the broadcast, along with a supplement by Colonel Andrews. Now, Alpha Centauri had become a place to live; a place with a name. There was a planet waiting, a well-developed planet; maybe more than one. Clearly the project could go ahead. He had received several communications from various countries wanting to know the procedures for bidding on different parts of *LITTLE ONE*. All wanted to know the time-line for the completion of the project.

A selection process began to assemble the largest body of engineers since Apollo to design *LITTLE ONE* for a historic voyage to take 1212 giants, their Counselors, and a number of their children back to the stars.

Iapetus – Saturn System

The four-ship Armada approached the entrance tunnel once again. Mentar and Brock rode Guppy 1. Kronos and Nycron asked to stay aboard Discovery and began reading the story of the building of Zannia 2, the starship also known as Iapetus. Guppy 2 followed with an empty cargo bay and a crew dressed and prepared to retrieve and collect all that might be discovered in the starship's Command Center; all that would be deemed important to the giant's journey home. Shuttles One and Two flew fore and aft of the Guppies.

The open pressure gates passed by silently, marking the miles. Forty minutes from the entrance of the tunnel they were hovering before the closed gates to what was surmised to be the central control for Zannia 2. Jake carefully touched down, checked Mentar and Brock's readiness for exit, then depressurized the cargo bay and opened the outer doors. Mentar and Brock went straight to the manual cranking system. Mentar grasped the hand-hold, then, gripping the crank, he began to turn it. A crack appeared between the doors and they began to slide away from each other. Minutes later they were full open. J.D. positioned Shuttle One to illuminate the tunnel. It went about a hundred yards into the outer shell of the starship and made a right turn. Mentar and Brock began walking toward it. The Armada followed. When the giants made the turn they encountered a huge open cavern with multiple seating and a continuous viewing screen that was a semicircle of one-hundred-eighty-degrees in the command center. Apparently, when the ship was active, there was a full panorama of the star field ahead of the ship.

The Armada of four ships flew into the bridge area and watched Mentar and Brock walk the full semicircle of seats facing the view screens. When they came to the two dominate center seats there were duplicate controls at the Pilot's seat and the Co-pilot's seat. The screens were larger than their counterparts filling the semi-circle of equipment.

Marvin, scanning the panorama of the bridge layout, envisioned perhaps a dozen members of the bridge crew seated in their respective seats monitoring the ship's status and the unfolding drama ahead. Perhaps three or four seasoned spacefarers standing, looking over the shoulders of a young trainees, patiently instructing them in the handling of the space ark on its way to—where? A mile away, inside the rotating part of the ship, a civilization, in transit in their inside-out world, going about their daily business, caring and being cared about. Perhaps stories being told to the children by the elderly; stories about living on the outside of a planet where you could look up and see the stars.

His mind came back to the moment. "Mentar, do you see anything that might help?"

Mentar went down on one knee, reached under, and pulled a cover off the front of the pilot's console. He followed the wiring harness and light tubes coming out of the bottom of the controls. All the communication lines went to a four-by-four by six-foot box mounted on the floor under the console.

Jim Blalock, watching Mentar through Guppy 1's windshield, reached over and released the restraining strap holding one of his diamond saws in place. He picked it up and checked the battery power reading. 100%. He checked his air supply on his suit. Dennis and Zeke did the same. They each got their helmets ready, then waited.

Mentar unplugged the lines and tubes from the enclosed metal box containing the electronics then tried to pick it up. It was secured to the floor of the bridge.

Jim, Dennis, and Zeke walked to the end of the cargo bay of the guppy. Jake looked across the way toward Shuttlecraft One. "Colonel, my crew's ready to cut the electronic package loose for Mentar.

Mentar turned and nodded, then pulled the cover off the copilot's console as well.

"Go ahead and get them both," Marvin said.

The crew of Guppy 1 made short work of cutting the anchors loose on the two control computers and loaded them into Guppy 2's cargo bay. They returned to the console, picked up the diamond saw and reentered Guppy 1, restored the tool to its restraining strap, then reentered the cabin of the ship.

Mentar examined the bridge again, searching the sides of the chamber beyond the view screens. There was an opening with the same doors blocking it. He stepped to the opening mechanism and cranked them open. It was a tunnel that lead off the bridge. He and Brock walked down the tunnel, following their shadows created by the Armada's lights. In about a hundred yards, on the right, on a lateral line with the bridge, was another chamber. They stepped into it and waited for the lighting from the ships. When the two shuttles entered the room was flooded with light.

The chamber was a hundred-yards square and about a hundred feet high. There were shelves on all the walls and two five-sided racks spaced in the middle of the room. All were loaded with electronic components of all shapes and sizes.

Marvin whistled. "There's millions of dollars right here."

Mentar spotted four more computer packages just like the ones retrieved and now in the guppy. Mentar and Brock picked up two each and approached the guppy. Maggie opened the cargo bay doors. They slid the four new units into the guppy. Mentar held up one finger in a 'standby gesture'. He hurried back to the rack and picked two more similar, but smaller, boxes and placed them into the guppy, then nodded to Maggie. She closed the doors.

Mentar and Brock walked around the room for several moments then stopped and turned toward Shuttlecraft One. "Colonel, we are finished here if you are satisfied."

Marvin paused a few moments. "So are we, however, there's one more thing I want to do for the best information for President Howell. I want to record on camera this room and, mainly, I want to fly and record the entire 360 degrees of the rotating cylinder at fifty-miles altitude for a permanent record. Lucas, while Mentar and Brock are reentering Guppy One, circle this room and image all these components on your recording equipment, then store it."

Lucas positioned Shuttlecraft Two fifty feet from the wall, began recording images, then circumnavigated the entire chamber and stored the information.

"Okay," Marvin said, "let's go back to Discovery, have a meal, restock, then take all eight ships into the cylinder, position them at fifty-mile intervals across the face of the cylinder, fifty-miles high to cover all the surface area of the cylinder, then fly the full circle. It will be about a four-hour mapping flight. That way, when we get back to Earth, a study sequence can be made of the montage we've recorded."

The four-ship Armada returned to Discovery. The valuable bounty in Guppy 2's cargo bay was moved to Discovery's. The crews had come to appreciate the faint gravity provided by the world-sized starship even though it wasn't enough to challenge even the weakest muscle born and conditioned on planet Earth. Soon, in a matter of hours, they would feel the familiar tug of *one-g* provided by Discovery's engines, once they are given the go-ahead.

Marvin informed Daniel and his team to load telemetry for a return to Earth. Departure in eight hours. The crews of all excursion craft were assigned the final task of completing the final mapping flight of the interior of Iapetus. A sense of urgency swept through the crews even though they would not see Earth for a little over a month. However, they were about to set sail for that special destination; Home, Sweet, Home.

Daniel gathered with his team at the navigation computers. His mind went briefly back to the evening on Mars when Javienne, a giant, had sung a ballad in Moon. Everyone was mesmerized with the apparent galaxy-wide sentiment. He must find out the words to the song that was written on Zannia, a planet circling another star. He would ask Javienne or Karen, or both for a translation in English. Right now, he must instruct

Discovery to go there. Discovery needed a map; in zeros and ones.

All eight excursion craft, recording equipment at the ready, entered the access tunnel of Zannia 2, the ancient starship, the yin-yang moon, Iapetus, for the final time. After today, all who were interested could see this marvel of construction and example of courage, anytime they wanted to view it. The ships proceeded cautiously, deliberately controlling the urge to hurry, finish, and head for home. A simple mistake here in this environment could be deadly.

The Armada followed the original route left of the central axis, straight to the side wall of the rotating cylinder, now quiet and still. Then they went left and toward the outer rim. They entered the inside world of the mechanism then descended to fifty-miles altitude above the surface of dwellings. The Armada held at this point and then had Shuttles Two through Guppy 2 fly laterally across the 'sky' with the crafts, by ascending numbers, stopping at fifty-mile intervals.

At the completion of the maneuver the eight ships were spread across the cylinder with a camera view that would include the full 400-mile-wide living surface below.

"Okay, ladies and gentlemen, cameras on, set your altitude at fifty miles, your speed at 250 miles per hour." All crafts responded with *"ready."* Marvin counted down and the four-hour recording session began; one of the greatest shows ever for primetime TV back home on Earth.

Chapter 22

GRAVITY

President Howell read the communication forwarded from NASA. He looked at his watch. Discovery had lifted off the surface of Iapetus half an hour ago. However, because of the great distances involved, it would be over a month before he could sit down with the crew and enjoy discussing the mission first-hand. Also, he anticipated with wonder the imagery of the interior of Zannia 2, a starship large enough to relocate a civilization from one planet to another.

The value of the derelict Colossus had been established, as expected. Now, the building of a starship was the next logical step. Ironically, the construction of planet Earth's first interstellar ship would not be for mankind's quest for the stars; but a transport for members of another civilization to return to the stars and their home.

However, some benefits came from this development. Number one: It could be done. That was the big one. And secondly: A better understanding of what it takes to actually succeed.

When *LITTLE ONE* was complete, stocked, and launched to the stars; Earth would bide the passing years until the magic number of twenty-six-and-a-half had arrived, give or take a few months, then the ship's designers would know for real if their work was successful. All 1216 travelers, plus their offspring, would be betting their lives on it.

Aboard Discovery – Exiting the Saturn system

"It feels like I've got weights strapped to me," Doug said. "I'd just about gotten used to near-weightlessness, and the weightless periods inside Zannia 2."

"It will go away in a few hours," Roger said. "The body quickly reverts back to its basic orientation. The bridge of Zannia 2 was designed into the non-rotating part of the ship. While piloting the ship, they would be weightless."

Doug, flexing his arms slowly, trying to get the imaginary weights off them, glanced at Roger. "They probably rotated bridge crews often to maintain everybody's physical tone."

Karen, Jean, Professor Liggins, and staff, were working on translating the regular-size, reader-type, books, retrieved from Zannia 2, into English. A textbook written as a tool to teach the young ones of civilization's most important endeavors; how to grow food. Karen took some deep breaths, working on shaking off the exaggerated feeling of weight. "It's after 9:00 p.m. on the world of Discovery and on our home still a month away. Tonight, which we will arrange by turning the lights down low, we can get a good night's sleep; being back in gravity's familiar arms."

Jean smiled. "I'm looking forward to that."

Marvin, about to turn in and get some sleep, went upstairs to visit with Mentar, Brock, Kronos, and Nycron for a few minutes. He saw the large growing-pots, ten feet in diameter, sitting near the wall of Deck 4. "Mentar, do you plan to make the trip back to Zannia with all your people awake during transit?"

Mentar sat down at the conference table. Marvin climbed the few steps and seated himself as well. Mentar glanced at the planter pots then back to Marvin. "We are discussing that both ways. We can afford the years to make the journey all awake and aware. However, food consumption is an issue. We will have to do some testing while *LITTLE ONE* is under construction to check yield. We could use half the ship for growing food and plants that produce oxygen. The issue on the food will be yield—of course. We prefer to be awake and aware.

Marvin nodded. "Twenty-two years inside a ship, even with an internal volume of seven billion cubic feet, is a long time."

"We thought of that. It would be similar to our tenure on the moon. We were enclosed in a sealed environment there, quite a bit larger. However, we could not just open the gate and walk out. Besides, Brock and I discussed the premise of the students taking classes transmitted from Earth. We could produce an academic atmosphere to occupy the students as the days and weeks passed." We, in turn, could transmit a daily report on how the mission is going and maintain a continuing communication with Earth."

"How about designing the ship to generate enough food and oxygen for all to travel awake and aware, yet have enough of the animation equipment and gas with you to put up to half of the ship's population asleep. Perhaps you should consider both. For example, you could let the couples stay awake that have children at that time. They can rear their children and run the ship. Just some things to think about," Marvin added. "Good night."

Marvin headed back down the stairs and to his quarters, to a bed that now was subject to gravity.

Discovery, taking aim at the fiery heart of the Solar System, sailed on.

Giant City, Kansas

Meta and Mingee, supervising the transfer of the student population from the temporary dwelling to the now completed housing complex, paused to welcome Dwight Cummins, special liaison from the president's office. Dwight, carrying a six-foot long document tube, followed them into the newly finished community center. They ascended a special ramp with seating arrangements, thoughtfully added by Mentar, and opened the document tube. He removed two rubber bands off a rolled-up drawing, six-by-ten feet, and spread it out on one of the tables. "This is a first draft of the ship Mentar is looking for. Admittedly it's a very early schematic of how the ship will be configured. The president asked me to stop by and show it to you. He wanted you to know that we are working on the project."

Meta and Mingee studied the schematic with interest. "Mentar and Brock will need to see this."

"I know," Dwight replied. "I'm going to leave this with you and I'll be back as soon as they arrive."

Dwight exchanged pleasantries with the giants and left.

NASA's think tank – Houston

NASA, commissioned by the president, began the process of selecting a location to build the colossus, *LITTLE ONE*. A starship four times the size of Discovery. New criteria had to be considered. The ships launched from this new location were not subject to equatorial considerations. Ships powered by Magnetic Inertial Propulsion did not have to contend with escape velocity, orbital speeds, or any of the precise sciences necessary for rocketry. Therefore, other considerations could take priority. Supply lines, weather, central location, and considerations that the building arena, when the ship was finished and launched, could become a space center for future space activities.

A stone's throw from Giant City, Kansas was the perfect choice. A section of land centrally located, plenty of room for the necessary facilities, and, a conveniently-sized workforce nearby for job one of the newly commissioned spaceport; the construction and launch of *LITTLE ONE*. A project requiring a launch pad a half-mile square.

When the surveyors showed up for the preliminaries, Meta and Mingee sent a dispatch to Discovery informing Mentar, Brock, Kronos, and Nycron of the growing excitement brewing in Giant City, Kansas. They also informed Mentar that a preliminary schematic of the layout of *LITTLE ONE* was waiting for him.

DAN HOLT

Chapter 23

THE ANOMALY

Discovery sailed on toward the rocky planets of the Solar System. Next up, the Asteroid Belt. So, Discovery's personnel prepared the ship for a possible AVS avoidance maneuver. So far there had been only minor trajectory changes. However, the ship would avoid a catastrophic collision even if the result was a several-G force. Larger bodies were avoided well ahead of time. Things very small would likely hit the ship with minimal or no damage. It was those in between that were of serious concern. They could cause such strong lateral movement that one could be seriously injured of even killed by a collision with the seats, consoles, fixtures, or struts inside the ship. All would be strapped in their seats securely until the danger was past.

With the boundary of the Asteroid Belt ahead, the radio came alive with a call from Navigation. Colonel Andrews keyed the radio. "Go ahead, Navigation."

"Colonel, we've picked up an object ahead, off the port bow, that appears to be artificial! It's about

150 feet across and about 40 feet thick. It is disc-shaped, Sir. It has a clean echo. I believe it's artificial."

"How far?"

"Three hundred miles."

"We can't stop to check it out traveling at this velocity. We'd be thousands of miles the other side of it by the time we got this ship stopped. Log where it is and send the information to NASA. Later, we'll come and check it out. It just might be what we haven't seen so far in all of this ordeal—one of their ships."

"If it is; it's a very small one, for them."

Frank scanned the port bow through the massive windshield. He could not see an object that small at three hundred miles like electronic radar equipment could. He might get a glimpse of it as they passed by, depending on how far off Discovery flight path the artifact was.

Frank noted that when viewing the Asteroid Belt from within, it seemed that it wasn't there at all. The celestial bodies occupying it, orbiting the Sun, were so far apart, an average of a million miles on a side, that actually seeing one was rare. If you studied the realm doggedly you might see a tiny dot of a sizable member of it far in the distance.

Finally, the Asteroid Belt was on the rearview monitors and the Mars orbit ahead. The planet had rounded the corner on its way to the far side of its orbit. With the Mars orbit traversed, ahead the Moon was standing to one side to clear the way for Discovery's return from a taxing and delightful mission. Onboard were treasures beyond expectations and discoveries that would challenge the scientific community for many years to come.

With the landing at Earth Base two hours away, Marvin went to his quarters, opened his carryall and picked up a small decorative gift box containing a diamond studded engagement ring and looked at it again. When he had gone shopping for a copy of Gulliver's Travels, the book store wasn't his only stop. He had radioed a private message to Al Billington a week ago to make some special arrangements. He slid the ring box into his pocket. The original crew of Research One had been clued in; with Roger being informed as well and participating in a special recording.

Earth Base – Aurora, Illinois

The seventy-two-day Mission had been a long one. The number of directly-involved people waiting at Earth Base just about matched the number arriving shortly. Families, friends and loved ones had gathered early for the landing of Discovery just before noon. They were visiting together, expressing gratitude and delight at having their crew home safe and sound. They knew that Discovery had been meticulously constructed as a massive mother ship to protect its compliment as a safe transport through the harsh reality of space. However, when she left the bonds of Earth and entered the Cosmos, she was very small indeed. When she gently deposits those nine landing struts on the landing pad at Earth Base, then the inner tension and concerns would go away.

The president and his entourage, the NASA administrator and his staff, and the security personnel added a twenty percent increase to the waiting crowd. Additionally, several hundred of the faithful had shown up and were waiting outside the cordoned off area adjacent to the landing pad to watch the never tiring spectacle of mother ship gracefully touching down on it landing pad. Military personnel were present and posted.

Jake and crew, upon Discovery's landing, manned Guppy 1, exited the Guppy bay and landed the excursion craft next to the open ramp of Discovery to provide transportation of Mentar, Brock, Kronos, and Nycron to Giant City, Kansas.

Renee Blanchart, Marvin's girlfriend, Sandra Gordon, Frank's wife, Isaac and Telma Henson, retired safety officer of the original Research One and his wife, Al and June Billington, a member of the ground crew of the original Research One, and his wife, waited as a group for the bridge crew. A welcome home party had been arranged.

The president began with, "I'll be brief so you can be with your families," and then finally tore himself away from the moment forty minutes later. That moment breathed new life into the weary travelers and the separate parties and get-togethers were arranged and began.

The Breakfast Fork Café – Aurora, Illinois

"This place is still the same," Isaac said.

Frank looked around the establishment. "Some things and places are timely. This one is a winner."

Karen and Jean were discussing the mission with the other ladies; answering the many questions, and describing the awesome scenes in the Saturn system.

Al stood. The group gradually got quiet. "Before we order and get this party underway, I want you to hear a recording that was recently made that will have a special meaning to all of us."

Al set a small recorder in the middle of the table, paused a moment, looking face to face, then pushed *Play*. Marvin's voice came from the recorder.

"Colonel Roger Stahls, this is Colonel Marvin Andrews. I have a very important question I want to ask you."

"Go ahead, Colonel, I'm listening."

"Sir, may I have your daughter, Renee's, hand in marriage?"

"Yes, you may. Take good care of her."

"Yes, Sir, I will."

Renee's eyes snapped to the recorder, then to Marvin's face. Her hands went over her mouth. Marvin stood, moved his chair out of the way, pulled the ring box out of his pocket, then went down on one knee. He opened the ring box. "Renee, will you marry me?"

"Yes!" Her arms went around Marvin's neck and then she kissed him.

The girls swarmed Renee to see the ring.

Chapter 24

THE PLAN

NASA's engineering department worked out the specifications of a starship capable of supporting 1200 giants, the equivalent of 8000 humans for twenty-two years while in transit to Alpha Centauri.

The final design would be half a mile in diameter and a quarter of a mile high. There were twelve decks. Four of them with one-hundred-foot ceilings to be used for plant growth, a forest of sorts, for oxygen generating flora. All other decks at fifty-foot ceilings. The bottom two decks were the engine room, housing 150 rotor pods and thirty backups plus spare parts storage.

Next was the main deck, containing the bridge, labs, medical, lounges, records, and communications. The next deck was personal quarters, recreational areas, and research areas. A constant streaming of academics would be beamed from Earth for the benefit of the Zannians.

All other decks would be dedicated to the cultivation and growth of food along with having a sitting area here and there; places to stop and sit for a while during an afternoon walk.

It would be a flying world, the only one the children would know, until arrival. At which time they would be men and women and would have their world turned inside out. When *LITTLE ONE* finally opened her outer doors and lowered her ramp onto the soil of Zannia they would walk out of her under a very big sky. A sky with two Suns.

As the months rolled by, complete drawings were generated and the allocation of the construction of the multiple segments of the ship began. The world was abuzz with international commerce.

The president and congress appointed a special oversight committee of oversee *LITTLE ONE's* construction contracts and the awesome task of transferring the great volume of bounty from the Saturn system to Earth.

Several companies petitioned for contracts to retrieve the bounty waiting on Iapetus in the Saturn system. They would arrange financing and build cargo ships, patterned after Discovery but with ninety percent of the ship's volume dedicated to cargo transport. A company was selected and began construction of two cargo ships. The salvaging of

Zannia 2 would span decades and would greatly enrich the bottom line of Earth's global economy.

Winston Stone, NASA administrator, petitioned Discovery's bridge crew for a planning meeting for the recovery of the anomalous object discovered in orbit in the Asteroid Belt. Its signature had indicated that there was a strong possibility that it was one of the giant's ships. Perhaps one that had been abandoned during the disaster event that occurred. NASA could not pass up an opportunity to learn its secrets.

Discovery could reach it in four days. Although the object was too large to fit through the entranceway of Discovery's cargo bay, it could be secured to Discovery's landing struts if they were left in the down position. The engineers saw no problem with that. The landing gear would be disabled in the down position and locked until Discovery returned with its bounty it had been removed from its tethered position. NASA mounted two reels of nylon straps, one on each of two of the second tripod gear set. They would pay out enough strap to reach to the third strut of the same set of struts, thereby securing the anomaly to Discovery. The reels would hold the object against to the inner-most set of struts until the ship hovered at a designated drop off area and the reels were released.

Discovery's crew had been back on Earth four months. NASA set launch for the new mission the following Monday; four days away. Marvin, among his friends, stated that he and Renee would be honeymooning in the Asteroid Belt. Shortly after they were married, Renee went into training with NASA on space flight. She, during her early years, was a journalist. Ships Records, Robert W. Sheridan, had met Renee and wanted her to become a part of Discovery's staff by joining his department. She had been an integral part of the space effort from the start. She had been the ground crew of the original space venture. She had agreed and put her Uncle Jason in an assisted living facility, a place he knew in Wichita, Kansas where several of his friends lived. She sold her Uncle Jason's business for him and began the process with NASA. She would be aboard upon launch. Renee was one of the fortunate that rode the vomit comet several times without a problem. A good physical trait. Her first space flight would be nine to ten days long with at least a day at *Zero- G.*

Mentar and Brock were notified and would be prepared for pickup before launch. As a team, they would capture the object and secure it to Discovery. They would be protected with a two-hundred-foot tether each and would be secured to the Guppy during the exercise.

Chapter 25

THE SHIP

Discovery lifted off with its basic crew plus Mentar and Brock. The usual precaution was taken the first 25,000 miles of flight. One day, relatively soon, that step can be taken out of the picture when the entrepreneur, that's sure to come, goes about building his business and clearing the skies of orbiting leftovers.

Discovery, now clear of the debris, settled into a four-day transit time to the strange anomalous object that had joined the asteroid belt many thousands of years ago. The radio came alive. A call from NASA.

"This is Discovery, go ahead," Marvin responded.

"Colonel," Winston said. "I just received a recording from Dwight Cummins, the president's liaison to the giants. Last evening, the giants had a concert on the launching pad for LITTLE ONE. All the giants were there and several hundred of our people. Dwight recorded it. Javienne played several songs. Then he played and sang a special number. Key in your intercom and take a listen. This is the song he sang on Mars, this time done in English."

Marvin keyed in the intercom enabling all aboard to hear. The rich sound of Javienne's instrument filled the ship. Momentarily the vocal began:

Home, home, that special place
Where you always belong
Home, home, that special place
Where you're always known

Though I sail among the stars
And many shores I roam
The Cosmos whispers gently to me
There's no place like home

Yeah, I search for glory on high
To know an exotic Race
Then I find at search's end
There's only one special place

Home, home, that special place
Where you always belong
Home, home, that special place
Where you're always known

There was an interlude where the instrument repeated the lead-in, in depth and purity and then the voice resumed.

I climb for the peak ahead
And strive to hold my own
Once again my thoughts come clear
There's no place like Home

At life's mountain high
I scanned my field of view
The message came from near and far
There's only one place for you

Home, home, that special place
Where you always belong
Home, home, that special place
Where you're always known

The vocal faded into silence, then the instrument slowly became quiet with Javienne holding the last chord.

After a few moments of silence Winston's voice followed: "How about that, Colonel."

"The giants will have him singing his way to Alpha Centauri."

"He's definitely up for the job."

"You'd better have the designers put a concert hall on that ship."

The Asteroid Belt

Discovery slowed to station-keeping at the coordinates supplied by NASA's computers. Marvin instructed Discovery to rotate in place. Minutes later they spotted the metallic oblong dot a half a mile away. Marvin eased Discovery toward it, slowly matching its orbital path and speed.

"Launch both Guppies and Shuttles One and Two. First, stop the oscillation, then I can bring Discovery in close so you can manually nudge the ship into place. Two people in each Shuttle and two in each Guppy suit up in addition to Mentar and Brock. All personnel suits checked, in your air locks ready, and tethered."

Mentar and Brock picked up a hand thruster each and a safety strap for each to attach them to their suits. They did so then entered Guppy 1. The eight other excursion members followed suit. All of them were armed with maneuvering thrusters for the job in *Zero-G*.

All four ships exited Discovery and positioned themselves in a semicircle around the now easily identifiable saucer. Jake opened Guppy 1's cargo bay. Mentar and Brock, outfitted with two-hundred-foot tethers, would approach the vessel and attempt to stop the tumbling motion. The vessel was tumbling in the direction of its orbit, as it were walking around and around the Sun. Mentar arrived first at the ship, reached up and attempted to block the ship's rotation. It pushed him away; however, it did slow the oscillation. Mentar stopped his drifting away from the ship. Next, Brock exercised the same maneuver further slowing the rotation. The next time Mentar met the body of the ship, he got it stopped and stable. Marvin eased Discovery to within ten feet of the ship and held. The rest of the crew exited their ships and collectively they coached the vessel up against the center tripod gear set. Brock and Mentar each got a strap and played it out from the reel to reach the third strut and secure the ship. When finished, they returned to Discovery.

Daniel engaged the telemetry and Discovery was on her way home.

Marvin went up the stairs to Deck 4. Mentar was scanning the books found on Mars.

"Mentar, do you recognize the ship?'

"Yes. It's a small personal craft. Seats four. I saw a hole in the hull. Looks like it was hit with debris and abandoned. It's empty. Apparently they had time to suit up and get picked up by another ship. I was reviewing these books to see if I could find any references to this ship. Colonel, you remember the raised platforms we investigated inside the ship at Solaris 6, ah, Saturn? That ship we just recovered would fit perfectly on those platforms."

"Yeah, it would," Marvin agreed. "Do you know how the engine works?"

"No. I rode in one of the personal ships once and I asked about it. The pilot said he wasn't an authority on it but understood that the principal was the stacking of gyroscopic forces. You know, when you try to push a gyroscope over, it automatically oscillates around another axis. They stack that effect by offsetting a wheel from its axis of spin, then mount another wheel inside that one, also offset from the center of spin. Then they oscillate the cluster of wheels. Somehow it comes out with a total force that's greater in a single direction."

Your engineers at NASA will figure it out. They are sharp. They worked out the structural bracing necessary for *LITTLE ONE* to be able to support its own bulk, fully loaded with hundreds of tons of supplies for our journey.

NASA Research Center – Houston

Discovery hovered over the tarmac in front of a spacious building designated to house the craft from another star. Guppy 1 powered up and transported Mentar and Brock to the ground level. They would enter the ancient ship and manually lower its landing gear so Discovery could release it. Mentar entered the ship, located it manual override, and cranked the gear to the down position. Discovery, responding to voice instructions descended to within six inches of the concrete. The NASA team released the restraining straps and allowed the personal craft to settle on the tarmac.

Discovery rose from its hovering position, moved to a clear area and touched down. Marvin lowered the entrance ramp and the bridge crew hurried down the ramp and to the recovered craft to take a look at the bounty. They each viewed the wheel clusters in the four corners of the ship with curiosity.

Frank, viewing the clusters, imagined marker boards covered with mathematical formulas with engineers and mathematicians studying them at length looking for that golden set of numbers that says—*yes*. His personal vigil, Frank thought, had been elusive, but then, one day, there it was, and the rotor pod was born. "They will find the answer," he thought.

Chapter 26

LITTLE ONE

The scaffolding alone created over a thousand new jobs. *LITTLE ONE*'s topmost hull was a quarter of a mile above its launching pad. Take all the scaffolding used on the capitol building, the statue of liberty, the vehicle assembly building at the cape, and the collection of shining skyscrapers of Mumbai, combine it together, then multiply it several times, and the scope of the construction becomes evident.

The twenty-four main beams of *LITTLE ONE* began arriving by ship. Each beam was a rugged latticework structure sectioned in sixty-foot pieces, twenty-two of them, that, when assembled, constituted a single main beam from center of mass to the edge of the ship. There was a total of 528 sections; twenty-four fully assembled beams. The basic frame had twelve complete beams on the bottom half of the ship and a matching twelve on the top, spread thirty degrees apart.

From a distance the giants looked like ants crawling through the forest of struts and bracing of the scaffolding, slowly making the frame of their ticket home come together. They could be heard humming to themselves as they busily went about their tasks.

Mentar, Meta, Kronos, and Mayan would begin a careful vigil of stocking the ship for departure to Zannia. Brock, Mingee, Juno, and Noon would keep the assemblers and the suppliers, plus the advising engineers and Little Ones on the same page during the construction process.

At this point, Mentar and associates would go about the lengthy process of assembling the supplies and appointments to be loaded on board the ship in about five years; the estimated completion date for *LITTLE ONE.* Their first act would be return to the Moon and deliver a memorial, designed by the survivors of the ancient disaster, to those who were lost; still entombed in the underground collective sarcophagus on Luna. The inscribed pillar would be placed at the entrance of the underground room for all who venture there to see. The caption on the top face would read: *"YOU WILL NOT BE FORGOTTEN,"* and would be signed by Mentar on behalf of the entire giant population. Below, on the four sides of the pillar will be inscribed the names of the 400 that were lost.

While on the Moon, Mentar would retrieve enough of the planter boxes, that were being used by the students to grow food for the elderly in the lunar arcology, to sustain the giants on their way home. The boxes had been discovered in the secondary tunnel in the lunar lab.

Aurora, Illinois

Discovery rose from its launch pad and entered a familiar highway to the Moon. This jaunt would seem short and simple indeed compared to the last two missions handled by America's starship. The one to Mars; seven times the hours of accelerated flight, and, especially the Mission to Saturn, a hundred and sixty times the flight duration.

That is, it would seem short and simple to all but Walter Howell. His second term had ended a few months ago. Senator James Whitmore had run for the White House and won easily with Howell's endorsement and his credentials, namely; he had chaired the first oversight committee that funded Discovery and its excursion craft. He ran on the premise of being the best versed on America's new stimulus—space flight.

Most of Walter Howell's advisors had been picked up by the Whitmore administration including Dwight Cummins. Dwight promptly informed the new president that there were three more giants in a family way; total now—six. Also, the appropriate-sized doctors were coming along just fine in medical school.

When Walter Howell left office he was asked to head up the salvaging of Zannia 2, the ancient spaceship in Saturn orbit. He accepted the position and promptly joined NASA's training program. He decided he wanted some feel of what the ships would be doing under his leadership during the decades long salvaging operation. The scheduled Moon Mission, being the less tense opportunity, was chosen as his introduction to space activities.

A relatively-strong AVS avoidance maneuver during exiting Earth's debris field left over by the earlier launches of many rockets was his first real notice that space is a serious place. But, when Discovery cleared the first 25,000 miles and things smoothed out, ex-president Howell, enjoyed his first space-borne round-table with his colleagues in Discovery's aft lounge. Marvin lifted his glass: "A toast to the man who rode out the beginning years of our new space program in the White House." They all jointly took a sip of their drinks.

"Speech, Speech!!" Came from around the table.

Walter Howell stood. "I've never told anybody this, but, I've sat in the oval office many hours and envisioned that I was on the Bridge of Discovery watching the stars stream by."

Doug smiled. "They don't stream by like on Star Trek."

"They did while I was on the Bridge."

"I understand," Doug agreed.

"If I freak out during midpoint turn around and reversal of power, just make sure I'm strapped in and give me a barf bag."

"You'll be fine," Dave said. "You'll be busy watching the stars stream by." There were random chuckles around the table.

Discovery settled on the lunar surface at its previously selected landing area. A meeting was assembled to review the ceremony about to take place. Discovery's excursion craft would set up a television link to Earth for the benefit of the giant population and all participants in the space program who wanted to be part of a dedication to those that were lost in the horrible disaster suffered by the giants of Zannia.

The Dedication

The giants on Earth, working on *LITTLE ONE*, suspended operations and gathered around their TV monitors to view the upcoming dedication to be conducted by Mentar. He would plant the pillar before the sea of containers, the resting place of those who lost the bid to survive.

Shuttles One, Two, Three, and Four, followed by Guppy 1 with Mentar, Meta, Kronos, and Mayan on board along with the dedication pillar that had been meticulously engraved with the names of those lost, left Discovery and headed for the tunnel into the lunar lab. At the entrance of the tunnel, the Armada paused long enough for Dave, suited and ready, to change the battery of the transponder and check its operation. Then the dedication group proceeded along the tunnel until they reached the enlarged section. One ship stopped and stationed itself there as a link. The other proceeded to the lower level where ship number two remained, then the remaining two shuttles continued into the secondary tunnel to the opening that led to the sea of sarcophagi waiting in solitude. The video link was established and checked.

Then Shuttle One's camera slowly swept the sea of 400 containers forever entombed on the Moon. Then the video equipment was focused on the scene of the guppy sitting on the floor adjacent to the chamber.

The doors of the guppy's cargo bay slowly opened and the four giants, with a carrying harness, lifted the dedication pillar and placed it at the entrance to the burial chamber. The giants removed the carrying harness and put it back into the guppy's bay then positioned themselves, four abreast, at the pillar. They were silent for a few moments, then Mentar, speaking in Moon, spoke for almost a minute. Then the four of them spoke three words in unison, then became silent and still for a full minute.

The dedication ended and the giants entered the guppy and the Armada returned to Discovery. Something special had just happened and Marvin and crew decided to leave it alone.

"Colonel," Mentar said across the meeting table, "each Guppy will hold a hundred of the planter boxes. The boxes stack inside each other. We need 4000 of them to outfit *LITTLE ONE*."

"That's twenty hours, ship time, for the two guppies; we can do that. Also, let's have Shuttle Three and Four in attendance. Go ahead with that Mentar. Meanwhile, I want to take Shuttles One and Two and search around the outside of the lab complex and see if we can locate the storage of that special sleeping gas. It's here somewhere and it's got to be a sizable storage area like the mound of the stuff we discovered on Mars."

Mentar set up the detail to obtain the planter boxes from the secondary tunnel and move them to Discovery's cargo bay. The four giants suited up; Mentar and Meta stayed in the planter box room to load the guppies and Kronos and Noon positioned themselves in the cargo bay to unload. The effort went smoothly. Each two hours, the crews returned to Discovery with the payload and changed their oxygen supply, then returned to resume the vigil.

Shuttles One and Two launched and began a systematic search for the moon gas. The first circumnavigation of the complex yielded nothing. They proceeded in an ever widening pattern, looking for any indication that there was an underground chamber of a larger size. Then, on the far end of the lab complex, the opposite end from the crater that had exposed the tunnel eons ago, there was a square shaped impression on the surface. Marvin ascended to 5000 feet to get a look at the overall picture. It was a distinctive square-shaped impression about two miles on a side; a four square mile *crater*—square-shaped. Near the middle of it there was an impact site. The crater resulting was about a hundred feet deep and two hundred feet across.

"That's got to be the reservoir of the gas," Marvin said. "That impact caused the roof of the chamber to collapse."

Doug looked toward the lab complex in the distance. "That impact is probably responsible for the interruption of the gas supply to the 400 that perished. By chance, the 1200 were spared. Their supply continued until we arrived."

"It's going to take major excavation to recover that supply," Frank noted. "If Mentar is going to make use of it, we'll have to go to Mars and get it."

"We've got to go back to Mars before they leave anyway," Dave said. "They are going to need some of the supplies stored there for when they do arrive at Zannia."

"Gentlemen," Roger said, "do you realize that you are looking at a stockpile of a special ingredient for almost unlimited reach toward the stars."

"Yeah," Marvin answered. "The only thing though, if you are going farther than Alpha Centauri, you would need to say your final goodbyes. When you return, if you choose to, everyone you knew would be gone."

DAN HOLT

Chapter 27

THE CARGO SHIPS

Discovery returned to Earth with 4000 pieces of furniture, a vital inclusion in *LITTLE ONE's* appointments. The calendar marched on as the construction continued. The blood in the business vein—money—was flowing profusely through the economy. Snyder General Systems, Richard James, (Dick) Snyder, owner and CEO, touched the necessary bases to win the contract to provide the conveyance of all the bounty to come to Earth from Saturn. Funding was arranged and two vessels were very quickly planned and construction began.

Discovery's prints were complete. All that was needed was a change in internal fixtures to allow maximum cargo capabilities. A simplification that expedited the building process. The two cargo transports could be constructed and ready for duty in just under two years.

That time had passed and the two newly completed ships were undergoing shakedowns for certification. Each would be complimented with six guppies with enlarged cargo bays; 20 x 30 x 50 feet, and two Shuttlecraft.

Following certification of all craft, their first assignment would be to accompany Discovery to Mars to retrieve supplies that Mentar and company wanted on board *LITTLE ONE* when she set sail for the stars. *LITTLE ONE* was now two years away from completion. It was not uncommon to see dignitaries from various nations riding golf carts across the expansive main deck, a half mile, looking upward at a quarter mile high ceiling in awe. The multiple fixtures looked new and normal until you got close enough. Then, they were seven times too big. For some. But not for those that would pray she take them home.

Snyder General Systems chose a location still known as Giant City, Illinois for its new branch, Space Services, Inc. Snyder was fond of that particular location because just across the highway was Discovery's home base, Earth base, and know-how. A construction and launching pad 1000 x 2000 feet was constructed for the building of the two ships and now for launching. Massive receiving and storage buildings were constructed adjacent to the landing pad.

A contract was awarded to Gordon and Gordon Magnetics to supply the six Guppies and two shuttles for each ship. NASA supplemented that work order with an additional two ships; shuttles for *LITTLE ONE*. They would be duplicates of Discovery's shuttles multiplied by seven; giant-size, having a diameter of 160 feet and would seat six giants. They were completed and delivered to Giant City, Kansas. The giants now had personal transportation around planet Earth.

In a televised ceremony, soon after the two massive cargo vessels were certified for space flight, the two ships were dubbed, with a champagne christening, the Maxie Gene and the Mary Lou. With the stage set and the ships ready, a Mars Mission was scheduled for six weeks away. Mentar and his team, in round-table meetings with NASA's planning team, generated a loading manifest for *LITTLE ONE*.

LITTLE ONE did not have the massive volume of Zannia 2; therefore, only the critical could be included on board for the journey home, four and a half lightyears away. A quarter of the ship's volume would be dedicated to water and all the equipment necessary for total reclaim.

NASA arranged a substantial storage of seeds in case Zannia was barren of food growth upon their arrival. Also, a hundred tons of US Army rations with a twenty-five-year shelf life were on the manifest.

Hopefully, neither would be needed. The giants had the equipment, the acreage, and the latest textbook on food-growing. More than likely, the toughest thing to combat would be the seemingly endless transit time. Twenty-two-years inside a world a half a mile across. Of course, there would be Earth television. Although, after so long a time, some of the content may inspire some to wish to abandon ship. Fortunately, there were four professional counselors on board. There would be the daily academic broadcast, Javienne's music, and each other. Not to mention several children to keep up with as they explored their *contained* world.

Chapter 28

MAN MADE MOUNTAINS

The newly trained bridge crews of the Maxie Gene and Mary Loui were flight checked again by Discovery's seasoned bridge officers. NASA assigned three trained pilots to each of the new ships for a period of six months as a prudent safety precaution.

Jake and Maggie, guppy pilots, spent hours training and checking out pilots for the super guppies, the enlarged copies of Discovery's guppies, that were specifically designed for moving bulk cargo. Pilots and crews for the new shuttles were selected and trained for escort duty on the two cargo vessels.

Aurora, Illinois – launch day

The three man-made mountains; Discovery, Maxie Gene, and Mary Lou, sat in a configuration at Earth Base and, just across the highway, at Space Services, Inc., awaiting the clock for launch. From the air they almost matched the layout of the three pyramids of Giza just outside Cairo, Egypt; Mankind's first bout with truly massive construction. Practice?

The transit time to Mars had grown to 36 hours and some few minutes. The guest-list of the original voyage petitioned for inclusion in this mission for additional experience and because of the thirst to *fly*. They were admitted and spread equally on the three ships. Mentar, Brock, Meta, and Mayan were aboard Discovery. They selected eight more of the giants from the pool that had flown to Mars earlier, four each for the Maxie Gene and the Mary Lou. They would need them for the loading of the freighters.

Ex-President Howell had gotten the bug as well and was aboard the Mary Lou, his ship, he was in charge of the salvaging operation. Oddly, Richard Snyder, soul owner and CEO of Snyder General Systems was aboard Discovery, although he owned the Maxie Gene and Mary Lou. He said this Mars Mission would be the only opportunity to look out a window and see his ships sailing the sea of space. He also had a team of three specialists in making documentaries for recruiting purposes.

The clock said *"yes"* and the three ships rose majestically in unison from Aurora, Illinois. At five thousand feet, following special programming, they sought and found each other's transponders and aligned themselves a thousand feet apart, then synchronized their acceleration. They all homed in on the computer generated thread that led to the red planet. Ninety rotor pods were doing what they were born to do and the ships sailed on. The first 25,000 miles went by without a hitch, the belts came off and the travelers, to the man and women, went to the port holes to view the other two ships. There was something mesmerizing about them. At mid-point turnaround they would do a special four-minute ballet. Maybe Javienne could write and produce something appropriate for that four-minute interlude.

Mars orbit

The Armada closed in on the red planet. The Maxie Gene had to dodge Phobos with a minor lateral move but quickly regrouped and settled in with the Armada at 1800 miles above the red sands below. The three ship underwent a thorough review of their systems and status of the same, especially the two on their maiden voyages. Cleared and ready, the three ships descended to the surface. Olympus Mons promptly reminded the Armada of its smallness. With the afternoon hours still available before the sun would set, Marvin chose to continue on with the flight until they were at their intended place of business; the vast storage of supplies that the ancient giants had stockpiled for this very journey.

They flew over the face as the new travelers stared in awe, then on to the structure, and on to the north side and landed three abreast before the entrance. The Sun, approaching the horizon behind the ships projected their shadow hieroglyphics on the walls of the pyramid shaped structure just yards away.

The Armada settled in for the night. Communications notified Houston of their arrival time and status of the Armada. Additional information was forthcoming as the Mission progressed.

Mentar radioed a message to the terminal at Giant City, Kansas; the radio system that was now housed in its completed structure where it would remain until it was installed on LITTLE ONE at departure. There it would keep Earth apprised of LITTLE ONE's journey to the stars. NASA television: The giant's saga; part 2.

Tomorrow morning the vigil would begin of selecting supplies by order of importance and ferrying them aboard the two freighters until capacity was reached. The crews made their ways to the lounges and the evening meal and camaraderie. The new crewmembers were still adjusting to the one third gravity of Mars.

Marvin and his bridge crew sought out Richard Snyder out of curiosity. He was discussing making a recruiting tool for use in the huge endeavor of salvaging Zannia 2. When he saw Marvin and crew approaching, he waved his documentary team away for the evening. He shook hands with Marvin and nodded to the others. They joined him around the table.

Marvin made the formal introductions although he was sure that Richard had met most of the crew if not all of them during his becoming involved in the saga of the giants. "Richard, I'm curious; how did you come up with the names of two ships that you have constructed for the salvage operation? I expected to see names like Salvage One and Salvage Two or something on that order. The names you chose are distinctive.

"I thought about that. However, there were two people that greatly influenced my life when I was entering the business world. One, Maxie Gene, a very influential person, opened a door for me which gave me an opportunity to use my skills. The other, Mary Lou, is my wife who never tires of telling me that I was good enough. I finally believed her.

Marvin nodded. "Well, their names are now forever etched in stone. It's an appropriate honor."

Chapter 29

SUPPLIED

Mentar, Meta, Kronos, and Mayan, entered Guppy 1 with their pressure suits prepped and ready and were flown into the structure. Maggie followed with her crew suited and bearing lifting ropes and harnesses in Guppy 2. Jake landed at the head of the aisle and opened the cargo bay doors. The giants exited the ship and began studying the listings of contents on the crates and picking the ones to be loaded into the ships.

The super guppies of the Maxie Gene and Mary Lou powered up along with the two shuttles and entered the structure. The new pilot and crews of the excursion craft stared at the half-mile-high stacks of shipping crates in awe. Although they had practiced many hours maneuvering the machines they now flew, they soon learned that a loaded guppy, in one-third gravity, required special attention and concentration. The many trips to and from the huge cargo ships quickly honed their skills.

Mentar pointed out three crates that were marked, in Moon: Farming equipment. Maggie flew to the upper stack of crates and hovered over a designated one. Her crew quickly secured it to the guppy. She lifted it clear of the stack and lowered it to the floor. The giants promptly loaded it into the super guppies. An efficient routine was quickly established. The stacks of crates got shorter and the cargo bays began to fill. When each guppy was filled, they headed for their respective ships and were unloaded by the giants on board.

The teams repeated the process, pausing every two hours for replenishing the suits, until the Sun crossed the sky. At the end of daylight, they retreated into their respective ships for the night.

The recovery of the bounty took four days. At the end of the vigil, a very exhausted team, reentered their ships, ready to return home.

When all vessels and personnel were safely back inside their respective ships, Marvin planned a quiet night for everyone to rest up. However, the swirling of the red dust just outside the windshield caught his attention. He checked visually side to side of the ship. "Dust storm. I think we're are seeing the beginnings of a dust storm. Some of those rage on for months, even years."

"What are we going to do?" Doug said.

"Leave now," Marvin stated, "right now, before we get caught in a dangerous storm. We are parked very close to a ground structure. We've got to leave while the atmosphere, what there is of it, is still calm."

Marvin signaled for the ships to launch immediately; countdown to commence in five minutes, launch on *zero*. Altitude: 1800 miles. First order of business; fly above the thin atmosphere and hence above the dust storm. Then the telemetry people can load telemetry for an immediate return to Earth.

Discovery, with the Maxie Gene and the Mary Lou, rose above the apex of the mile-high building, climbing for the sky. In the distance the bridge crews saw a wall of red dust, a half-a-mile high, rolling in their direction. The Armada quickly left it far below.

DAN HOLT

Chapter 30

TO THE STARS

The three ships settled back onto their launch pads at Aurora, Illinois. The two ships, the Maxie Gene and the Mary Lou, would be unloaded into Snyder General's mammoth warehouses. The Zannia-bound variety of goods and supplies would wait there until *LITTLE ONE* was completed, tested, and declared space worthy. Then, the mountain-sized craft would appear at the docks and open its cargo bay doors to receive the tools it would need to rebuild a civilization.

The days rolled by at America's third spaceport, it's creation following behind the Cape, then Aurora's Earth Base, and now, just outside Wichita, Kansas; The Frank Gordon Space Flight Center. The outside scaffolding had disappeared from around the saucer shaped mountain of aluminum and special alloys. Now contained, the real design work began. Building for space flight. Everything must remain viable in *Zero-G*, a condition that would be a routine aboard this craft with its unique form of propulsion. Although the *Zero-G* condition would always be brief, they would be part of life on the ship. You could set your watch by them as they were for the purpose of velocity control. Over the weeks, months, and years, the episodes would be a break from a, perhaps sometimes, boring day; even relished by some as part of a game of amusement.

Agricultural labs around the country were testing growth of various foods under the conditions of *LITTLE ONE's* environment. All the growing pots from the Moon were cleaned, examined, and tested for function. They were equipped with spring loaded mechanisms that, when they became weightless, they automatically closed, like a flower closing its petals for the night, to capture their contents. Then, when gravity was restored, they would open and resume as usual.

Five more giants had given birth and four more were on the way. Ironically, as they entered the world; a world borrowed; their world, for at least the first twenty-two years of their life, was being constructed outside. Perhaps in their society, many years from now, however you count years with two Suns crossing the sky every day, they would be known as *The Transits* or, perhaps, *The Earth Born*.

Departure

The Bonneville Salt Flats, for one last time, was the focal point of space activities. Well-announced, well-attended, well-supervised for safety of the public, it could brag over two million people in attendance. Suspended above the forty square mile flats at 500 feet, were thirty spaceships powered by Magnetic Inertial Propulsion. The largest was *LITTLE ONE,* a half a mile across, with two excursion craft nestled on each side of her, each 160 feet across. Next, there was Discovery, 600 feet across, with her eight excursion craft circling her, each 24 feet across. Then the Maxie Gene, 600 feet across, with her eight excursion craft, also 24 feet across, and finally the Mary Lou, 600 feet across, with her eight excursion craft 24 feet across.

Following today's ceremony, three of the spacecraft would be lost to another star.

Speeches were made, regrets voiced, a brief history outlined, then a special moment: *LITTLE ONE,* with its two shuttles, was stationed in the center of the Armada. Following a moment of silence when the vocal ceremonies were concluded, the two excursion craft of *LITTLE ONE* flew to their docks above the massive windshield, paused as the hangar doors opened, then entered the mother ship, and the doors closed.

There were moments of silence. Then, Shuttlecraft One, originally, Research One, ascended to the piloting level of the huge *LITTLE ONE* and approached the windshield, stopping 10 feet away. Marvin keyed the radio; a link that included all the spacecraft and a PA system arranged for all on the ground to hear.

"Goodbye, my friend. I will miss you."

"Goodbye, little one, thank you and planet Earth for saving our lives and helping us get home. We won't forget. Wait for my call.

Mentar keyed the mike once more: "Launch in ten seconds."

Chapter 31

THE PICTURE

Twenty-six and a half years later

The Maxie Gene and the Mary Lou passed each other in Jupiter space, one going, one coming, as they continued the chore of salvaging Zannia 2 in Saturn orbit.

The older, seasoned pilot, hanging on to the youthful endeavor of space flight one more year, flying the Maxie Gene, keyed the radio upon visually sighting the Mary Lou passing by two miles away. "Have you heard the news?!"

"What news?"

"They made it!"

"Who made it?"

"Mentar and the giants."

"Oh, yeah? Wow! I remember them. I was twelve when they left. They made it, huh?"

"Do you have anybody onboard over there that's over 50?"

"Yeah, one of our cooks."

"Let me talk to him."

Charles Powell heard the young pilot of the Mary Lou on the intercom: "Cookie to the bridge, cookie to the bridge, you have a phone call."

"This is Cecil Monahan," came from the radio.

"Cecil, this is Charles Powell, piloting the Maxie Gene. How old are you?"

"Fifty-six, Sir."

"Cecil, what are you doing sailing through space at fifty-six years old?"

"Well, Sir, my wife, Judy, passed away five years ago and I just feel closer to her up here."

"I see. I just wanted to let you know about the news that just came in at NASA. Mentar and the giants made it to Zannia."

"That's great!" Cecil responded. "I liked Mentar; he was a great guy. He was a big *drink of water* but a great guy."

"You met Mentar?"

"Well, I didn't actually meet him. When they were moving from Illinois to Kansas, the wife and I drove down to the designated route they were walking to see them. I messed around and got my car into a ditch. Mentar, when he was walking by, saw my problem. He simply reached down and pushed it back upon the road."

Marvin, Doug, Dave, Roger, and Daniel were standing at the ramp of Research One with Frank Gordon. The ship, recreated in its original form, was sitting in Frank's driveway. They were waiting for Isaac Jacob Henson, 92, to arrive for the up and coming flight to Houston, to NASA's headquarters.

A van entered the driveway and stopped. The right-hand door opened and the seat floated out the door, then the safety override engaged and the rotochair sank to within six inches of the driveway. Isaac steered via the controls to move to the group. Doug glanced at the logo on the back of the chair. Rotochairs, Inc. The appliance had a basketball sized rotor pod under its center, compliments of Gordon and Gordon Magnetics.

Isaac's caregiver, Alice, came walking from around the van shaking her finger at Isaac. "You are supposed to wait for me before you exit the vehicle in case something goes wrong."

Isaac nodded. "Alice," Isaac said, "have you ever been in a flying saucer?"

"Yes. My son has one."

The group of seven men plus Alice entered Research One, lifted off, and began the flight to Houston.

"When did the message come in?" Doug asked.

"Three days ago," Frank responded. "It's accompanied by a picture that tells it all."

Research One settled on the concrete pad just outside NASA headquarters. The group disembarked and entered the building. A representative was waiting to guide them to the conference room.

NASA's receiving equipment that had been trained on Alpha Centauri for the past several months had captured the signals in their entirety and reproduced them on a six by eight-foot screen.

The group stared for moments in appreciation. On the screen was Mentar and the entire population of giants, including 36 children. Behind the group was a pristine space elevator reaching into the heavens, disappearing out through the top of the picture. Further, there were two Suns, one on each side of the latticework tower, one considerably brighter than the other. The secondary one was about half the size as the other. The caption at the bottom of the picture read:

WE MADE IT, MY FRIENDS. WE ARE HOME.

END

ABOUT THE AUTHOR

Dan Holt is a U.S. Army veteran, having served three years as a Communications Specialist in Germany. He spent the remainder of his civilian career as a self-taught engineer, designing and testing large-scale production equipment for the file folder industry. The efficiency and durability of his designs even garnered interest from some foreign manufacturers.

In retirement, Dan has used his writing skills to express his continuing fascination with machinery and science fiction. His zest for adventure and intrigue continue to rule in his first novel, UNDERNEATH THE MOON and in the sequel, UNDERNEATH THE MOON 2. Now, this 3rd book in the Underneath The Moon Trilogy brings the adventure to a conclusion.

His variety in sci-fi thought is evident in his other novels, SLEEP MODE and KEEPSAKE. Underneath The Moon, Sleep Mode and Keepsake are all now available on audio through www.audible.com. Underneath The Moon 2 in in audio production and UTM3 will begin production soon, due out in October 2016. See all of Dan's books at www.maxholtmedia.com.

www.ingramcontent.com/pod-product-compliance
Lightning Source LLC
Chambersburg PA
CBHW061552170626
46811CB00001B/178